Gregory Mcdonald

Confess, Fletch

Gregory Mcdonald is the author of twenty-five books, including nine Fletch novels and three Flynn mysteries. He has twice won the Mystery Writers of America's prestigious Edgar Allan Poe Award for Best Mystery Novel, and was the first author to win for both a novel and its sequel. He lives in Tennessee.

Books by Gregory Mcdonald

Fletch
Fletch Won
Fletch, Too
Fletch and the Widow Bradley
Carioca Fletch
Confess, Fletch
Fletch's Fortune
Fletch's Moxie
Fletch and the Man Who

Son of Fletch
Fletch Reflected

Flynn
The Buck Passes Flynn
Flynn's In

Skylar
Skylar in Yankeeland

Running Scared
Safekeeping
Who Took Toby Rinaldi? (Snatched)
Love Among the Mashed Potatoes (Dear Me)
The Brave

Exits and Entrances
Merely Players
A World Too Wide
The Education of Gregory Mcdonald (Souvenirs of a Blown World)

Gregory Mcdonald

Confess, Fletch

Vintage Crime/Black Lizard
Vintage Books
A Division of Random House, Inc.
New York

FIRST VINTAGE CRIME/BLACK LIZARD EDITION, MARCH 2002

Library of Congress Cataloging-in-Publication Data
Mcdonald, Gregory,
Confess, Fletch / Gregory Mcdonald.
New York: Vintage Books, 2002.
p. cm.
ISBN: 0-375-71348-4
1. Fletch (Fictitious character)—Fiction. 2. Private investigators—
Massachusetts—Boston—Fiction. 3. Art thefts—Fiction.
4. Boston (Mass.)—Fiction.
PS3563.A278

www.vintagebooks.com

Printed in the United States of America
10 9 8 7 6 5 4 3 2 1

TO

Judy and Lew, Susie and Chuck, Stuart,
Karen and Rupert, Jennette and Alan,
HoRo, HoHo, Susi, Chris and Doug

I

FLETCH snapped on the light and looked into the den.

Except for the long windows and the area over the desk, the walls were lined with books. There were two red leather wing chairs in the room, a small divan, and a coffee table.

On the little desk was a black telephone.

Fletch dialled "O".

"Get me the police, please."

"Is this an emergency?"

"Not at the moment."

The painting over the desk was a Ford Madox Brown—a country couple wrapped against the wind.

"Then please dial '555-7523'."

"Thank you."

He did so.

"Sergeant McAuliffe speaking."

"Sergeant, this is Mister Fletcher, 152 Beacon Street, apartment 6B."

"Yes, sir."

"There's a murdered girl in my living room."

"A what girl?"

"Murdered."

Naked, her breasts and hips full, her stomach lean, she lay on her back between the coffee table and the divan. Her head was on the hardwood floor in the space between the carpet and the fireplace. Her face, whiter than the areas kept from the sun by her bikini, eyes staring, looked as if she were about to complain of some minor discomfort, such as, "Move your arm, will you?" or "Your watchband is scratching me".

"Murdered," Fletch repeated.

There was a raw spot behind the girl's left ear. It had had time to neither swell nor bleed. There was just a gully with slim blood streaks running along it. Her hair streamed away from it as if to escape.

"This is the Police Business phone."

"Isn't murder police business?"

"You're supposed to call Emergency with a murder."

"I think the emergency is over."

"I mean, I don't even have a tape recorder on this phone."

"So talk to your boss. Make a recommendation."

"Is this some kinda joke?"

"No. It isn't."

"No one's ever called Police Business phone to report a murder. Who is this?"

"Look, would you take a message? 152 Beacon Street, apartment 6B, murder, the name is Fletcher. Would you write that down?"

"156 Beacon Street?"

"152 Beacon Street, 6B." Through the den door, Fletch's eyes passed over his empty suitcases standing in the hall. "Apartment is in the name of Connors."

"Your name is Fletcher?"

"With an 'F'. Let Homicide know, will you? They'll be interested."

I I

FLETCH looked at his watch. It was twenty-one minutes to ten.

Instinctively he timed the swiftness of the police.

He returned to the living room and mixed himself a Scotch and water at the sideboard. He would not bother with ice. He concentrated on opening the Scotch bottle, making more of a job of it than was necessary. He did not look in the direction of the girl.

She was beautiful, she was dead, and he had seen enough of her.

Sloshing the drink in his glass as he walked, he went back into the den and turned on all the lights.

He stood at the desk, looking closely at the Brown. The cottage behind the country couple was just slightly tilted in its landscape, as if it, too, were being affected by the wind. Fletch had seen similiar Browns, but never even a reproduction of this painting.

The phone made him jump. Some of his drink splashed on to the desk blotter.

8

He placed his glass on the blotter, and his handkerchief over the stains before answering.

"Mister Fletcher?"

"Yes."

"Ah, good, you did arrive. Welcome to Boston."

"Thank you. Who is this?"

"Ronald Horan. Horan Gallery. I tried to get you earlier."

"I went out to dinner."

"Your letter mentioned you'd be staying in Bart Connor's apartment. We did some restoration work for him a year or two ago."

"It's very good of you to call, Mister Horan."

"Well, I'm very excited by this Picasso you mentioned in your letter. You said it's called 'Vino, Viola, Mademoiselle'?"

"It's been called that. God knows how Picasso thought of it."

"Of course, I'm puzzled why you came all the way from Rome to Boston to engage me as your broker. . . ."

"There's some evidence the painting is in this part of the world. Possibly even in Boston."

"I see. Still, I expect we could have handled it by correspondence."

"As I wrote in my letter, there may be one or two other matters I'd like to consult you about."

"Yes, of course. Anything to be of service. Perhaps I should start by warning you that this painting might not exist."

"It exists."

"I've looked it up, and there is no record of it anywhere that I can find."

"I have a photograph of it."

"Very possibly it does exist. There are a great many Picassos in existence which have never been recorded. On the other hand, the body of Picasso's work very often has been victim to fakes. I'm sure you know his work has been counterfeited more than the work of anyone else in history."

"I do know, yes."

"Well, I wouldn't be giving you professional service if I didn't bring these matters up to you. If such a painting exists, and it's authentic, I'll do everything I can to find it for you and arrange for the purchase."

Rotating blue lights from the roofs of police cars storeys below began to flash against the long, light window curtains. There had been no sound of sirens.

"Are you free to come by tomorrow morning, Mister Fletcher?"

Fletch said, "I'm not sure."

"I was thinking of ten-thirty."

"Ten-thirty will be fine. If I'm free at all."

"Good. You have my address."

"Yes."

"Let's see, you're on Beacon Street across from the Gardens, right?"

"I think so."

Fletch pushed the curtains aside. There were three police cars in the street. Across the street was an iron railing. The darkness beyond had to be a park.

"Then what you do is this: leave your apartment and turn right, that is, east, and go to the end of the Gardens. Then turn left on Arlington Street, that is, away from the river. Newbury Street will be the third block on your right. The gallery is about two and a half blocks down the street."

"Thank you. I've got it."

"I'll send someone down to open the door to you at ten-thirty precisely. We're not a walk-in gallery, you know."

"I wouldn't think so. I'm sorry, Mister Horan, I think there's someone at my door."

"Quite all right. I look forward to seeing you in the morning."

Fletch hung up.

The door buzzer sounded.

It was seven minutes to ten.

I I I

"MY NAME'S Flynn. Inspector Flynn."

The man in the well-cut, three-piece, brown tweed suit filled the den doorway. His chest and shoulders were enormous, his brown hair full and curly. Between these two masses of overblown brown was a face so small it had the cherubic quality of an eight-year-old boy, or a dwarf. Even with the hair, his head was small in proportion to his body, like a tiny, innocent-looking knob in control of a huge, powerful machine. Nothing indoors had the precise colour of his green eyes. It was the bright, sparkling green of sunlight on a wet spring meadow.

Below the break of his right trouser leg were a half-dozen dots of blood.

"Pardon my pants. I'm fresh from an axe murder."

For such a huge chest cavity, for anyone, for that matter, his voice was incredibly soft and gentle.

Fletch said, "You're an Irish cop."

"I am that."

"I'm sorry." Fletch stood up. "I meant nothing derogatory by that."

Flynn said, "Neither did I."

There was no proffer to shake hands.

As Flynn vacated the doorway, a younger and shorter man came in, carrying a notepad and ballpoint pen. He had the grizzled head of someone fried on a Marine Corps drill ground a score of times, like a drill sergeant. The rubbery skin around his eyes and mouth suggested his eagerness to shove his face in yours, tighten his skin, and shout encouraging obscenities up your nose. In repose, the slack skin gave him the appearance of a petulant basset. His suit and shirt were cheap, ill-fitting, but spotless, and his shoes, even this late on a drizzly day, gleamed.

"This is Grover," said Flynn. "The department doesn't trust me to do my own parking."

He settled himself in a red leather chair.

Fletch sat down.

It was twenty-six minutes past ten.

He remained waiting in the den. A young, uniformed police-man waited with him, standing at parade rest, carefully keeping his eyes averted from Fletch. Beyond the den, other police, plainclothesmen, moved around the apartment. Fletch wondered if any reporters had sneaked in with them. Fletch heard the murmur of their voices, but caught nothing of what they said. Occasionally, a streak of light from a camera flashbulb crossed the hall, from either the left, where the bedrooms were, or the right, where the living room was.

An ambulance crew entered, rolling a folded stretcher across the hall, towards the living room.

"Close the door, will you, Grover? Then make yourself com-fortable at the wee desk there. We don't want to miss a word of what this boyo in the exquisite English tailoring has to say."

The uniformed policeman went through the door as Grover closed it.

"Has anyone read you your rights?" Flynn asked.

"The first fuzz through the door."

"Fuzz, is it?"

Fletch said, "Fuzz."

"In more human language," Flynn continued, "I ask you if you don't think you'd be wiser to have your lawyer present while we question you."

"I don't think so."

Flynn said, "What did you hit her with?"

Fletch could not prevent mild surprise, mild humour appearing in his face. He said nothing.

"All right, then." Flynn settled more comfortably in his chair. "Your name is Fletcher?"

"Peter Fletcher," Fletcher said.

"And who is Connors?"

"He owns this apartment. I'm borrowing it from him. He's in Italy."

Flynn leaned forward in his chair. "Do I take it you're not going to confess immediately to this crime?"

He used his voice like an instrument—a very soft, woodland instrument.

"I'm not going to confess to this crime at all."

"And why not?"

"Because I didn't do it."

"The man says he didn't do it, Grover. Have you written that down?"

"Sitting here," Fletch said, "I've been rehearsing what I might tell you."

"I'm sure you have." Elbows on chair arms, massive shoulders hunched, Flynn folded his hands in his lap. "All right, Mister Fletcher. Supposing you recite to us your opening prevarication."

The green eyes clamped on Fletch's face as if to absorb with full credulity every word.

"I arrived from Rome this afternoon. Came here to the apartment. Changed my clothes, went out to dinner. Came back and found the body."

"This is a dandy, Grover. Let me see if I've got it in all its pristine wonder. Mister Fletcher, you say you fly into a strange city, go to an apartment you're borrowing, and first night there you find a gorgeous naked girl you've never seen before in your life murdered on the living room rug. Is that your story, in short form?"

"Yes."

"Well, now. If that doesn't beat the belly of a fish. I trust you're got every word, Grover, however few of them there were."

Fletch said, "I thought it might help us all get to bed earlier."

" 'Get to bed', he says. Now, Grover, here's a man who's had a full day. Would you mind terribly if I led the conversation for a while now?"

"Go ahead," Fletch said.

Looking at his watch, Flynn said, "It's been a near regular custom I've had with my wife since we were married sixteen years ago to get me home by two o'clock feeding. So we have that much time." He glanced at the glass of Scotch and water Grover had moved to the edge of the desk blotter. "First I must ask you how much you've had to drink tonight."

"I've had whatever's gone from that glass, Inspector. An ounce of whisky? Less?" Fletch asked, "You really have inspectors in Boston, uh?"

"There is one : me."

"Good grief."

"I'd say that's a most precise definition. I'm greatly taken with it, myself, and I'm sure Grover is—an Inspector of Boston Police as being 'good grief'. The man has his humour, Grover. However, we were speaking of the man's drinking. How much did you have to drink at dinner?"

"A split. A half bottle of wine."

"He'll even define 'split' for us, Grover. A remarkably definitive man. You had nothing to drink before dinner?"

"Nothing. I was eating alone."

"And you're going to tell me you had nothing to drink on the airplane all the way across the Mediterranean Sea and then the full girth of the Atlantic Ocean, water, water everywhere. . . ."

"I had coffee after we took off. A soft drink with lunch, or whatever it was they served. Coffee afterwards."

"Were you travelling first class?"

"Yes."

"The drinks are free in first class, I've heard."

"I had nothing to drink on the airplane, or before boarding the airplane. I had nothing to drink at the airport, nothing here, wine at the restaurant, and this half glass while I've been waiting for you."

"Grover, would you make a note that in my opinion Mister Fletcher is entirely sober?"

"Would you like a drink, Inspector?" Fletch asked.

"Ach, no. I never touch the dirty stuff. The once I had it, the night after being a student in Dublin, it gave me a terrible headache. I woke up the next morning dead. The thing is, this crime of passion would be much easier to understand if you had a bottle or two of the old juice within you."

"You may find that is so," Fletch said. "When you find the murderer."

"Are you a married man yourself, Mister Fletcher?"

"I'm engaged."

"To be married?"

"I expect to be married. Yes."

"And what is the name of this young lady whose luck, at the moment, is very much in question?"

"Andy."

"Now why didn't I guess that myself? Write down 'Andrew', Grover."

"Angela. Angela de Grassi. She's in Italy."

"She's in Italy, too. Grover. Everyone's in Italy except he who has just come from there. Make a social note. She didn't come with you due to her prejudice against the Boston weather?"

"There are some family problems she has to straighten out."

"And what would the nature of such problems be?"

"I attended her father's funeral yesterday, Inspector."

"Ach. Dicey time to leave your true love's side."

"She should be coming over in a few days."

"I see. And what is it you do for a living?"

"I write on art."

"You're an art critic?"

"I don't like the words 'art critic'. I write on the arts."

"You must make a fortune at it, Mister Fletcher. First class air tickets, this lavish, opulent apartment, the clothes you're wearing. . . ."

"I have some money of my own."

"I see. Having money of your own opens up a great many careers which otherwise might be considered marginal. By the way, what is that painting over the desk? You can't see it from where you are."

"It's a Ford Madox Brown."

"It's entirely my style of work."

"Nineteenth-century English."

"Well, that's one thing I'm not, is nineteenth-century English. And who with a touch of humanity in him would be? When did you notice it yourself? The painting, I mean?"

"While I was calling the police."

"You mean to say, while you were calling the police to report a murder, you were looking at a painting?"

"I guess so."

"Then, indeed, you must be a most relentless writer-on-the-arts. I understand you used the Police Business phone to report the heinous deed rather than Police Emergency."

"Yes."

"Why is that?"

"Why not? Nothing could be done at the moment. The girl was clearly dead. I'd rather leave the Emergency line clear for someone who needed the police immediately, to stop a crime in progress, or get someone to a hospital."

"Mister Fletcher, people with stutters and stammers and high breathlessness call the Police Emergency number to report a cat in a tree. Did you look up the Police Business number in a book?"

"The operator gave it to me."

"I see. Were you ever a policeman yourself?"

"No."

"Just wondering. Something about your sophistication regarding bodies in the parlour. The conciseness of your answers. After a murder, usually it's only the policeman who want to get to bed. Where was I?"

"I have no idea," Fletch said. "In the nineteenth century?"

"No. I'm not in the nineteenth century, Mister Fletcher. I'm in Boston, and I'm wondering what you're doing here."

"I'm here to do research. I want to try a biography of the Western artist, Edgar Arthur Tharp, Junior. He was born and brought up here in Boston, you know, Inspector."

"I do know that."

"The Tharp family papers are here. The Boston Museum has a great many of his works."

"Have you ever been in Boston before?"

"No."

"Do you know anyone here?"

"I don't think so."

"Let's go over your arrival in Boston again, Mister Fletcher.

It makes such a marvellous story. This time, tell me the approximate times of everything. Again, I remind you that Grover will take it all down, and we're not supposed to correct him later, although I always do. Now: when did you land in Boston?"

"I was in the airport waiting for my luggage at three-forty. I set my watch by the airport clock."

"What airlines? What flight number?"

"Trans World. I don't know the flight number. I went through customs. I got a taxi and came here. I got here about five-thirty."

"I understand about going through customs, but the airport is only ten minutes from here."

"You're asking me? I believe Traffic Control is also considered Police Business."

The representative of Boston Police said, "Ach, well, so, of course it was five o'clock. Where in particular did you get stuck?"

"In some crazy tunnel with a dripping roof and chirruping fans."

"Ah, yes, the Callahan. I've sat in there myself. But at five o'clock the traffic in there usually gets stuck going north, not south."

"I shaved and showered and changed my clothes. I unpacked. I left here I would guess a little after six-thirty. I took a taxi to the restaurant."

"Which restaurant?"

"The Café Budapest."

"Now, that's interesting. How did you know enough to go to such a fine restaurant your first night in town?"

"The man sitting next to me on the plane mentioned it."

"Do you remember his name?"

"He never mentioned it. We didn't talk much. Just while we were having lunch. I think he said he was some kind of an engineer. From someplace I think called Wesley Hills."

"Wellesley Hills. In Boston we spell everything the long way, too. Did you have the cherry soup?"

"At the Budapest? Yes."

"I hear it's a great privilege, for those who can afford it."

"I tried to walk home. It had seemed like a short ride in the taxi. I left the restaurant shortly after eight and got here, I would say, just before nine-thirty. In the meantime, I got thoroughly lost."

"Where? I mean, where did you get lost?"

16

Fletch looked around the room before answering. "If I knew that, would I have been lost?"

"Answer the question, please. Describe to me where you went."

"God. A Citgo sign. A huge, gorgeous Citgo sign. Remarkable piece of art."

"There, now, you see, that wasn't so difficult, was it? You turned left rather than right. That is, you went west rather than east. You went into Kenmore Square. What did you do then?"

"I asked a girl for Beacon Street, and it was right there. I walked along it until I came to 152. It was a long walk."

"Yes. That was a long walk. Especially after a Hungarian dinner. So you came into the apartment, and went into the living room. Why did you go into the living room?"

"To turn off the lights."

"So you must have gone into the living room the first time you were in the apartment and turned on the lights."

"Sure. I looked around the apartment. I don't remember whether I left the lights on in the living room or not."

"Undoubtedly you did. Anyone as likely a murderer as you are is apt to do anything. Now, why were you in Rome?"

"I live there. Actually, I have a villa in Cagna, on the Italian Riviera."

"Then why didn't you fly from Genoa, or Cannes?"

"I was in Rome anyway."

"Why?"

"Andy has an apartment there."

"Andy-the-girl. You've been living with Andy-the-girl?"

"Yes."

"How long."

"A couple of months."

"And you met with Bartholomew Connors, Esquire, in Rome?"

"Who? Oh, no. I don't know Connors."

"You said this is his apartment."

"It is."

"Then how are you in it, if you don't know Mister Connors?"

"Homeswap. It's an international organization. I think their headquarters is in London. Connors takes my villa in Cagna for three months; I use his apartment in Boston. Cuts down on the use of money."

"You've never met?"

"We've never even corresponded. Everything, even the exchange of keys, was arranged through London."

17

"Well, I'm sure I'll catch up again with this world, one day. Don't write that down, Grover. So, Mister Fletcher, you say you don't know Bartholomew Connors at all, and you don't know Ruth Fryer either?"

"Who is she?"

"You answered that question so perfectly I'm beginning to believe I'm talking to myself. Mister Fletcher, Ruth Fryer is the young lady they have just taken out of your living room."

"Oh."

" 'Oh', he says, Grover."

"Inspector, I believe I have never seen that young lady before in my life."

"Taking your story as the word from John—that's Saint John, Grover—when you discovered the body, didn't you wonder where the young lady's clothes were? Or are you so used to seeing gorgeous girls naked on the Riviera you think they all come that way?"

"No," Fletch said. "I did not wonder where her clothes were."

"You came in here and looked at a painting, instead."

"Inspector, you've got to understand there was a lot to wonder about at that moment. I was in a state of shock. I didn't know where the girl came from. Why should I wonder where her clothes went to?"

"They were in your bedroom, Mister Fletcher. With the bodice torn."

Fletcher ran his eyes along a shelf of books.

"I'm not sure I've ever heard the word 'bodice' spoken before. Of course, I've read it—in nineteenth-century English novels."

"Would you like to hear my version of what happened here tonight?"

"No."

"Let me run through it, anyway. I can still get home in time for two o'clock feeding. You arrived at the airport, having left your true love in Rome, but also after having been confined to her company for two months, living in her apartment, the last few days of which have been sad days, seeing her to her father's funeral."

"Sort-of funeral."

"You escaped the dearly beloved with divine celerity, Mister Fletcher. That's a nice alignment of words, Grover. Have you got them all?"

"Yes, Inspector."

"In their proper order?"

"Yes, Inspector."

"You came here and introduced yourself to this huge, impressive apartment. Your sense of freedom was joined by a sense of loneliness, which is a potently dangerous combination in the loins of any healthy young man. You shave and you shower, spruce yourself up, never thinking ill of yourself for a minute. Are you with my version of the story so far?"

"I can't wait to see how it comes out."

"You take yourself out into the drizzle. Perhaps you do the obvious and stop in at the first singles bar you come to. You put forth your noticeable charm to the most attractive girl there, possibly a little under the drizzle from gin—by the way, Grover, we'll want to know what's in that girl's stomach—entice her back here, to your bedroom, where she resists you, for some reason of her own. She promised mother, or had forgotten to take her pills, or whatever it is young ladies say these days when they change their minds. You tear her clothes off her in the bedroom. Thoroughly frightened, she runs down the corridor to the living room. You catch up to her. She continues to resist you. Perhaps she is screaming, and you don't know how thick the walls are. You're in a new place. You left your fiancée this morning in Rome. Here's the classic case of adults in a room, and one of them isn't consenting. In frustration, in anger, in fear, in passionate rage, you pick up something or other, and knock her over the head. To subdue her—get her to stop screaming. Probably even you were surprised when she crumpled and sank to your feet."

Flynn rubbed one green eye with the palm of his huge hand.

"Now, Mister Fletcher, why isn't that the obvious truth?"

"Inspector? Do you think it is the truth?"

"No. I don't."

He pressed the palms of both hands against his eyes.

"At least not at the moment," he said. "If you'd been drinking —yes, I'd believe it in a minute. If you were less attractive, I'd believe it. What else do these girls hang around for, if it's not the Peter Fletchers of the world? If you were less self-possessed, I'd believe it. It's my guess it would take less cool to get rid of a resisting girl than go through an initial police questioning for murder. Never can tell, though—we all have our moments. If you hadn't called the Police Business phone, I'd be quicker to believe in your being in an impassioned, uncontrollable state. No. I don't believe it, either."

Grover said, "You mean, we're not arresting him, Inspector?"

"No, Grover." Flynn stood up. "My instinct is against it."

"Sir!"

"I'm sure you're right, Grover, but you must remember I haven't the benefit of your splendid training. I'm sure any experienced policeman would put Mister Fletcher behind bars faster than a babe can fall asleep. It's times like these, Grover, that inexperience counts."

"Inspector Flynn...."

"Tush, tush. If the man's guilty, and he most likely is, there'll be more evidence of it. If I hadn't seen the suitcases in the hall myself, I'd think the whole thing was a pack of lies. I suspect it is, you know. I've never met a writer-on-the-arts before, but I've not considered them such a randy subspecies before, either."

Fletch said, "I expect you're going to tell me not to leave town."

"I'm not even going to say that. In fact, Mister Fletcher, I'd find it very interesting if you did leave town."

"I'll send you a postcard."

Flynn looked at his watch.

"Well, now, if Grover drives me home, I'll be just in time for my cup of camomile with my Elizabeth and my suckling."

"I will, Inspector." Grover opened the door to the empty apartment. "I want to talk to you."

"I'm sure you do, Grover. I'm sure you do."

I V

EXPECTING the normal delays in completing a transatlantic telephone call, as well as the normal difficulty of getting Angela de Grassi on the phone any time of the day or night, Fletch made his effort while remaining in bed in the morning.

He was greatly surprised when the call went through immediately, and Angela answered on what appeared to be the first ring.

"Andy? Good noon."

"Fletch? Are you in America?"

"Arrived safely. Even you can fly to Boston and arrive in one piece."

"Oh, I'd love to."

"Are you eating lunch?"

"Yes."

"What are you having?"

"Cold asparagus with mayonnaise, a few strawberries. Have you had breakfast?"

"No. I'm still in bed."

"That's nice. Is it a nice bed?"

"Sort of big for one person."

"Aren't they all?"

"No. This bed kept me awake all night, calling out 'Andy! Andy! Where are you? We need you. . . .' "

"My bed asked for you, too. Is the weather good there?"

"I don't know. I can't see it through the fog. How goes the battle?"

"Not so good. I spent all day with the lawyers and the commissioner of this and the commissioner of that. We're never going to get this straightened out. All the legal officials tell us he's dead, we must consider him dead, adjust to it and go live our own lives. Which is why we had the funeral service. But the lawyers insist everything must be left up in the air until we know more. Remember Mister Rosselli? He was at Poppa's funeral Monday. Poppa's lawyer. Chief mourner. Very big with his handkerchief. A day later, yesterday, he's putting his hands in the air saying there's nothing they can do until more is known."

"What are you going to do?"

"Keep trying, I guess. Everyone's being very sympathetic."

"But nothing's getting done."

"I've always heard lawyers will fiddle around forever, milking an estate—is that the expression?—like a cow, until they have grabbed everything in fees and nothing is left. Even a little estate like my father's."

"Sometimes it happens."

"And Sylvia, of course, darling stepmother Sylvia, is acting her usual bitch self. She announces about every ten minutes that she is the Countess de Grassi. Every doorman in Rome must know she is the Countess de Grassi by now. I get to tag along like a poor waif."

"Why don't you forget about it all and come over here?"

"That's the point, Fletch. Everyone tells us we must adjust, accept the facts, and go back to living our own lives. But we can't do that without some kind of income from the estate. They've turned everything off."

"I don't see that it matters. You and I get married, and it doesn't matter how many years it takes to settle the estate. I mean, who cares?"

"I care. Listen, Fletch, I don't care how long it takes to settle the estate. I don't care about the rotten old house or the income. All I want is the will read. I want to know to whom the bulk of the estate goes—my father's third wife, or my father's only daughter. That matters to me."

"Why?"

"If it goes to Sylvia, fine. That's my father's prerogative. I would never contest it. So I'd lose my family's home. Okay, I can walk away from that. Never again would I think of the old servants as my responsibility. Remember, Fletch, Ria and Pep brought me up. If most of the estate goes to me, they're my responsibilities. Right now I can do nothing about them. Not even answer the questions in their eyes. They are my responsibility. Sylvia can take her precious countess-ship and walk into the sea with it."

"Andy, Andy, this is an emotional matter. Between two women."

"You bet it's an emotional matter. The whole situation is bizarre enough without everything being left up in the air this way. I don't care if the will is never executed, is that how you say? All I want to know is what the will says."

"I'm sort of surprised you can't get the substance of the will somehow out of Rosselli."

"This man! He dandled me on his knee when I was a baby. Now he will tell me nothing!"

"He's still dandling you on his knee."

"And Sylvia doesn't leave me alone for a moment. When she's not two paces in front of me announcing to the world she is the Countess de Grassi, she is two paces behind me trying to find out what I do. Every minute she asks, 'Where did Fletcher go? Why did he go there? What is he doing in Boston?' "

"What have you told her?"

"I said you went to Boston on personal business. Something about your family."

"Look, Andy. Don't forget why I am in Boston."

"And you'd better find them, Fletch. It's becoming very important. Even if Sylvia inherits most of the estate, she will never take care of the responsibilities. What's happened so far?"

"Horan, the man from the gallery, called last night. Almost the minute I arrived."

"What did he say?"

"He never heard of such a painting. I'm meeting him this morning."

"He says he never heard of the Picasso?"

"That's what he said."

"How did he sound to you?"

"What can I say? He sounded authentic."

"This is crazy, Fletch. At least you don't have Sylvia, the Countess de Grassi, to contend with."

"Listen, Andy, would you do me a favour?"

"Anything, Fletch of my heart."

"Will you go up to Cagna?"

"Now?"

"This guy, Bart Connors, who took the villa. One of us ought to have a look at him."

"Why? Isn't the apartment all right?"

"Yeah, it's fine. It's just that something has come up which makes me sort of curious about him."

"I'm supposed to drive all the way up to Cagna because you're curious about someone?"

"I flew all the way to Boston because you're curious about someone."

"Fletch, if I leave Rome, leave Rosselli and the other old baboons to Sylvia. . . ."

"Nothing will happen. My curiosity about Connors is more than casual, Andy. I need to know what sort of a person he is."

"Really, Fletch."

"Take the Porsche, take the train, fly to Genoa, rent a car, do whatever is easiest for you. You need to get away a day or two, anyway."

"Is that what you're really thinking?"

"No. I really want to know about Bart Connors."

"Your precious villa."

"You'll go?"

"Of course. How can I say no?"

"I thought you were saying no."

"I wouldn't think of it, darling. I'll leave my father's estate to wolf lawyers and vixen Sylvia, and fly to see if your tenant is happy."

"I'll appreciate it."

"Anything else I can do, Big Boss?"

"Yeah. After you look at Connors, come to Boston. Have you ever made love in the fog?"

"Fletcher, I have to straighten things out here."

"Forget it. The whole estate isn't worth a fart in a gale of wind. We can take care of your precious Ria and Pep."

There was a silence on the line.

"Andy?"

"I'll come as soon as I can, Fletch. Until then."

V

ACROSS the Charles River the Cambridge Electric sign, still lit, looked dull through the fog. Cars going along the highways on both sides of the river used parking lights or headlights.

After he shaved and took a cold shower, he did his hundred push-ups on the bedroom carpet, a towel spread under him.

Not dressing, he padded down the corridor.

The girl had run along here the night before. She had found herself in a situation she had had every right to think playful and fun but which suddenly went wrong, desperately wrong, hopelessly out of her control. She fled. Would she have fled the apartment naked?

Or was her running down the corridor, perhaps pretending to be frightened, part of her play?

In the living room, Fletch sat on the stool of the baby grand piano and stared at the spot where she had lain. The dim morning light, the shadows between the divan, beyond the coffee table, did little to alleviate the original shock of her presence, her smooth, sun-touched skin, the youthful fullness, leanness, shape of her body, the queer angle of her head, the discomfort in her face, her being dead.

Ruth Fryer. Ms. Fryer. Fletch knew more about her. She was about twenty-three. She had been brought up in health and self-confidence by loving parents. Boys, men had loved her. She had loved them, loved her freedom. She trusted. She had always been treated gently, considerately. Until last night.

Last night she had been murdered.

He went through the dining room, pushed open the swing door to the kitchen, and snapped on the light.

There was no milk or cream in the refrigerator, but there were five eggs and some butter. He would scramble eggs with water. Instant coffee was in a cupboard.

While he was scrambling the eggs he heard the old iron grille of the elevator door clang shut. Then he heard a key in a lock.

To his surprise, the swing door from the front hall opened.

In the door stood a woman, carrying a plastic shopping bag by its handles. Her eyes were wide-set and huge, her cheekbones high, her lips curiously long and thin. Her raincoat was open, loose. Around her hair was a red, blue and black bandanna. She was in her mid-fifties.

"Good morning," Fletch said, staring from the stove.

"I'm Mrs. Sawyer. I clean here Wednesdays and Saturdays."

"I'll try to remember."

"That's all right." Her smile was directed more at Fletch's confusion than his nakedness. "I run naked around my place, too."

"You arrive early."

"Don't apologize. I don't buy those magazines, but I'm not so old I don't enjoy seeing a naked man. 'Course, you aren't black, Honey."

Fletch took the fork out of the frying pan.

When he turned, she was standing directly before him, searching his eyes.

"Before I do anything," she said, "you answer me."

Fletch was not about to back against the stove.

"You kill that girl last night?"

Fletch answered her eyes. "No."

"You ever kill anybody, anytime?"

Fletch could not answer her eyes. "Yes."

"When?"

"In a war."

"All right." She put her shopping bag on the table. "Your eggs are burning."

"How do you know about it?"

25

"It's in this morning's *Star*. Mister Connors said to expect a Mister Fletcher."

"Do you still have the newspaper?"

"No. I left it in the subway." She took off her coat and laid it neatly across the table. "Here, give me that pan."

Fletch looked down at himself.

She said, "So old Anne Sawyer can still do that to young men. My, my. I'll remember that, Saturday night."

"Does Connors like women, too?"

"Oh, yes. Especially after his wife left him for another woman. There's been a parade through here. Everything but the brass bands and the fire trucks."

Fletch said, "I'll get dressed."

"Your eggs are ready. From your tan marks, I'd say you're not too used to wearing all that many clothes anyway, regular."

"I'll get dressed."

"Your eggs will get cold."

Fletch said, "I'm cold."

"All right."

V I

T H E eggs were cold. They were also watery.

Mrs. Sawyer had set a place for him at the dining room table.

He presumed the telephone was for Bart Connors.

Mrs. Sawyer pushed open the kitchen door.

"It's for you. A Mister Flynn."

Fletch took his coffee cup with him, across the dining room, through the living room, through the hall, to the den. He also took the hotel room key.

"Good morning, Inspector."

"Now who would this be?"

"Fletcher. You called me."

"Oh, yes. Mister Fletcher. I forgot who I was calling."

"Inspector, you'll be glad to know I passed a lie detector test this morning."

"Did you indeed?"

"Administered by a Mrs. Sawyer, who comes in to clean twice a week. She arrives very early."

"How did she administer it?"

"She asked me if I killed the girl."

"And I daresay you had the gall to say you didn't?"

"She stayed to do her work."

Flynn said, "I was reasonably startled when a live woman answered your phone this morning. I said to myself, 'What is this boyo we have here?' I thought of giving the woman some warning."

"Which makes me think, Inspector. Did your men find a key to this apartment among the girl's possessions?"

"Only a Florida driver's licence. And that was in her left shoe."

"No key? Mrs. Sawyer had a key."

"Cleaning ladies are apt to have keys. Girl friends aren't. But I take your meaning, Mister Fletcher. Other people might have keys to that apartment."

"Mrs. Sawyer found a key this morning. Just off the carpet in the corridor."

"A key to your apartment?"

"No. A hotel key."

"How very interesting."

Fletch looked at it in his hand.

"The tag on it says 'Logan Hilton—223'. How could your men have missed it?"

"How, indeed? It's possible, of course, they didn't miss it—that it wasn't there at all. The suicide note hasn't been found yet, either."

"What?"

"Isn't that the theory you're working on this morning, Mister Fletcher? That the young lady let herself into your apartment with her own key, undressed in your bedroom, went into the living room, and hit herself over the head?"

"I'm not working on any theory this morning, Inspector."

"I know you're not. You're just trying to be helpful. Even your defensive theories are peculiarly lame. I've never known a man so indifferent to a murder he might have committed."

"What did the driver's licence say?"

"That Ruth Fryer lived in Miami, Florida."

"That all? Is that as far as you've gotten this morning?"

"Plodding along, Mister Fletcher, plodding along. Today should turn up some interesting facts."

"I'll keep this key for you."

"We have turned up one curious fact already. I called customs officials this morning. You did arrive from Rome yesterday at about three-thirty. Trans World Airlines flight number 529."

"What's curious about that?"

"Your name isn't Peter Fletcher. The name on your passport is Irwin Maurice Fletcher."

Fletch said nothing.

Flynn said, "Now, why would a man lie about a thing like that?"

"Wouldn't you, Inspector, if your first names were Irwin Maurice?"

"I would not," said Flynn. "My first names are Francis Xavier."

VII

FLETCH hesitated at the corner of Arlington Street before turning left.

Walking along the brick sidewalk he turned up the collar of his Burberry. Lights were on in the offices of the brownstones to his right. After months of sun, the cool October mist felt good against his face.

He did not hesitate under the canopy of the Ritz-Carlton Hotel. He had seen the sign from a block and a half away. He went through the revolving door, across the lobby to the newstand and bought a map of Boston and a *Morning Star*.

Turning away from the counter, he saw there was a side door and went through it. He was on Newbury Street.

He turned the pages of the newspaper as he walked. The story was on page five. It was only three paragraphs. No picture. He was identified in the second paragraph as "Peter Fletcher" and was attributed with calling the police. The third paragraph said, according to police sources, he had been alone in the apartment with the murdered girl.

The bare facts made it seem he was guilty. And the Boston press did not care much about the story.

He knew. The only follow-up expected from such facts would

be the indictment of Peter Fletcher. Not much of a story. No mystery.

Classified advertisements were in the back of the paper, just ahead of the comics page. He tore out the strip concerning "Garages For Rent" and stuffed the rest of the newspaper into a small rubbish basket attached to a post at the corner. He put the piece of newspaper and the map in his coat pocket.

In the next block was the Horan Gallery. Of course, there was no sign. A building, an old town house, a thick, varnished wood garage door to the left, a recessed door with a doorbell button, two iron grilled windows to the right. The windows on the second, third and fourth floors were similarly grilled. The place was a fortress.

The brass plate under the bell button gave the address only —no name.

The door opened as Fletch pushed the button.

The man, in his sixties, wore a dark blue apron from his chest to his knees. He also wore a black bow tie with his white shirt, black trousers, and shoes. A butler interrupted while polishing silver?

"Fletcher," Fletch said.

To the right of the hall, in what had once been a family living room, was no furniture other than objects of art. Passing the door, Fletch saw a Rossetti on an easel. On the far wall was a Rousseau, over a standing glass case. On a pedestal was a bronze Degas dancer.

Going up the stairs, Fletch realized the house was entirely atmosphere-controlled. With thermostats every five metres along the walls, the temperature was absolutely even. The air was as odourless as if man had never existed. Few of the world's major museums afforded such systems.

The man, remaining wordless, showed Fletch into a room on the second floor and closed the door behind him.

Facing the door was a Corot, on an easel.

Horan rose from behind a Louis Seize desk, made a slight nod of his head which would have passed in Europe for an American bowing, and strode across the soft Persian carpet with his hand extended.

"I understand now," he said. "You're younger than I expected."

Horan hung Fletch's damp coat in a tight closet.

A Revere coffee service awaited them on a butler's table between two small, comfortable, upholstered divans.

"Cream or sugar, Mister Fletcher?"

"Just the coffee will be fine."

"I spent a pleasant half hour reading you this morning—your monograph on Edgar Arthur Tharp, Junior. I should have read it before this, of course, but it was unknown at the Athenaeum until I requested it."

"You do your homework."

"Tell me, was it originally done as a doctoral thesis? It had no university imprimatur on it."

"I did it originally about that time in life, yes."

"But you've only printed it recently? Of course, you're still not much older than the average graduate student. Or are you one of these people blessed by the eternal appearance of youth, Mister Fletcher?"

Horan was a far more attractive man than Fletch had expected. In his early fifties, he was slim but heavily shouldered. His features were perfectly even. Without wrinkles, his complexion had to have been cosmetically kept. Over his ears, his hair, brushed back, was silver, not grey. Hollywood could have sold tickets to films of him dancing with Audrey Hepburn.

"Of course," he continued after Fletch's silence, "I haven't yet gotten my enthusiasm up for the bulk of American artists. Cassatt, Sargent, all right, but your Winslow Homers and Remingtons and Tharp all seem so indecently robust."

"Michelangelo and Rubens you would not call robust?"

"The action in the work is what I mean. The action, the moment, in the bulk of American work seems so existential. It is overwhelmed by its own sense of confinement. It does not aspire." Horan tasted his coffee. "I shall leave my lecturing for my class at Harvard, where I am due at twelve o'clock. About this Picasso?"

Fletch said, "Yes."

Being offered a seat was one thing; being put in his place another.

"What is there to say about the work I haven't already said?" Horan asked the air. "It may not exist. Then again it may. If it exists, where is it? And can it be authenticated? Believe it or not, the job of authentication is easier, now that the old boy is dead. He was prone to claim works he liked, whether he did them or not, and to deny works he probably did do, if he didn't like them. Then, after we find it, there is the question of whether whoever owns the work is willing to sell, and for how much. You may have come a long way for nothing, Mister Fletcher."

Fletch said nothing.

"Or did you really come to Boston to expand upon your work on Tharp?"

"Actually, I did," Fletch said. "I'm thinking of trying his biography."

Horan's forehead creased.

"Well," he said. "If I can be of any help. . . . Introduction to the Tharp Family Foundation. . . ."

"Thank you."

"You want the Picasso purely for your private collection?"

"Yes."

"You represent no one else?"

"No one."

"There is the question of credit, Mister Fletcher. Most of the people I deal with, I've dealt with for years, you understand. Other than your monograph, privately printed. . . ."

"I understand. The Barclough Bank in Nassau will establish whatever credit for me you require."

"The Bahamas? That might be very useful."

"It is."

"Very well, sir. You mentioned you have a photograph of the Picasso?"

Fletch removed the envelope from his inside jacket pocket. He placed the photograph on the table.

"The photograph was made from a slide," he said.

"As I thought," Horan said, picking it up. "Cubist. And Braque did not do it." He tapped the photograph against his thumbnail. "But we don't know if Picasso did."

Fletch stood up.

"You'll make enquiries for me?"

"By all means."

"How long do you think it will be before you know something?"

Horan was following him.

"I'll get on the phone this afternoon. It may take twenty minutes, or it may take twenty days."

On a little table next to the closet door was a copy of the

New York Times. Fletch's notoriety had not penetrated the Horan Gallery. He looked at the front page.

"I never bother with the Boston newspapers," Horan said.

"Not even the society pages?"

Horan held his coat for him.

"I believe anything of sufficient importance to warrant my attention will appear in the *New York Times.*"

Horan opened the door. The houseman, still in his apron, waited on the landing to show Fletch out.

Fletch said, "I'm sure you're right."

VIII

APPARENTLY doing nothing but consulting his map, Fletch stopped across the street and looked at the Horan building.

On each side of the roof, along the lines where the building joined with roofs of buildings to its left and right, ran a high, spiked iron fence. Its forward ends curved over the edge of the roof, fanning halfway down the fifth storey. The windows on the third, fourth and fifth storeys were barred, too.

Ronald Horan liked his security.

Using his map, Fletch crossed to Boylston Street and walked into Copley Square.

There, at the State Street Bank and Trust Company—after long, albeit courteous, delays, interviews with everyone except the most junior teller, proving his identity over and over again, including showing his passport, listening five times to the apologetic explanation that "all this is for your own protection, sir"—he picked up the twenty-five thousand dollars in cash he had had sent ahead. He took the money in fifty and one hundred dollar denominations.

He observed how much easier it always is to put money into a bank than it is to take out. Even one's own money.

"That's what banks are for, sir."

"Of course."

Then he lunched on a tuna fish sandwich and Coke.

He taxied to five used car lots, in Boston, Brookline, Arlington, Somerville and Cambridge, before he found precisely the van he wanted. It was last year's Chevrolet, light blue, with an eight-cylinder engine, standard shift, heating, and air conditioning. He paid cash for it and had the garageman replace all four tyres. The garageman also obliged him by providing the legally necessary isurance for the van, through his sister-in-law, who ran an office across the street. The insurance bill was outrageous in relation to the cost of the vehicle.

Comparing the map with the list of garages for rent he had torn from the newspaper while going back to town in the taxi, he told the driver to go to the Boston underground garage. It was not far from his apartment. Once at the garage, he rejected it immediately—there would be no privacy there, typical of most government-run facilities the world round. He wanted walls.

He walked to a garage advertised on River Street, even closer to his apartment. First he woke up the housekeeper left in charge of the negotiation by its owner. She had to find the key. In broken-down, red house shoes, describing her osteitis in jealous detail, she showed him the garage. The monthly rent was exorbitant. But the place had brick walls and a new, thick wooden door. He paid two months' rent in cash and took the key, as well as a signed receipt (made out to Johann Recklinghausen) shortly after the interminable time it took the woman to find the receipt book.

He advised her to see a doctor.

After standing in line for forty-seven minutes at the Commonwealth and Massachusetts Registry of Motor Vehicles at 100 Nassau Street before being able to present his driver's licence, purchase agreement marked "Cash—Paid", and application for insurance, he was given his vehicle registration (for a light blue Chevrolet caravan) and two licence plates.

They attached his licence plates for him at the used car lot in North Cambridge.

Driving back into Boston, he stopped at a corner variety store and bought twenty-five issues of that evening's *Boston Globe*. The curiosity of the storekeeper and his wife made Fletch wonder if indeed he was mentioned in that evening's newspaper. In the van, he went through one newspaper quickly. He wasn't.

He also stopped at a hardware store and bought a quart of black paint, a cheap brush and a bottle of turpentine.

It was dark when he returned to River Street. Leaving the garage door open and the van outside with its lights on, he spread the *Globe* all over the cement floor.

Then he drove the van into the garage, on to the paper, and closed the door.

Being careful of his clothes, doing a purposefully messy job by the headlights reflected from the front wall, he climbed on top of the van and wrote, "YOU MUST BE HIGH" on the roof. Climbing down, again over the windshield, he wrote, in huge, dripping letters, on the left panel, "FEED THE PEOPLE". On the right panel, "ADJUST!"

As the truck was wet from the mist before he began, the mess he created was perfect.

After cleaning his hands with the newspapers and turpentine, he locked the garage.

Then he taxied to the Sheraton Boston Hotel and rented a two-door, dark blue Ford Granada Ghia, which he drove to his apartment and parked on the street.

I X

L I G H T S were on in the apartment.

Taking off his coat, Fletch went directly into the den. He flung the coat over an arm of a chair.

On the desk was a note for him.

It read, "Call Countess de Grassi at Ritz-Carlton—Mrs. Sawyer."

Aloud, Fletch said, "Shit!"

"Would it be more bad news for you, Mister Fletcher?"

Inspector Flynn was looking in at him from the hall.

"I fear we must add to it."

Grover joined Flynn from the living room.

"Your Mrs. Sawyer allowed us to remain after she left," Flynn said, "after we had fully proven ourselves not only Boston Police officers but fully virtuous men as well."

Fletch left the note upside down on the desk.

"If you want to talk to me, let's not sit in here," he said. "I got sort of tired of this room last night."

"Precisely why we were waiting for you in the living room." Flynn stepped back to let Fletch pass. "It's airier."

"Do you gentlemen want a drink?"

"Don't let us spoil your pleasure."

Fletch abstained.

He sat in one of the divans at the fireplace—the one nearer where the corpse had lain, and therefore not in view of the site.

"You've led us a merry chase," Flynn said, letting himself down in the opposite divan. "After you disappeared this morning, you would have found it impossible to leave the City of Boston —at least by public transportation."

"Disappeared?"

"Now you can't tell us you went in one door of the Ritz-Carlton and out of the side door in a flash, thereby dropping our tail on you, out of the purest of all innocence!"

"Actually, I did," Fletch said. "I just stopped in to buy a newspaper."

"Such an innocent man, Grover. Have we ever met such a blissfully innocent man? Here, stalwart men of the Boston Police have been staking out all the terminals all the day, the airport, the train stations, the bus stations, armed with the description of our murder suspect here, and our Mister Fletcher pops up at the cocktail hour like a proper clubman with the entirely reasonable explanation that he went in one door of a hotel and out of another simply to buy a newspaper!"

"I bought a map of Boston, too."

"We were just about to leave," Flynn said, "having heard you rented a car a half hour ago. A blue Ford Ghia, whatever that is—I suppose it's got wheels—licence number what-is-it, Grover?"

"R99420," Grover read from his notebook.

"By the by, Grover. Go call off that all-points-bulletin on that car. Let the troopers on the Massachusetts Turnpike relax tonight. Mister Fletcher is at home."

Grover returned to the den to use the telephone.

Flynn said, "Is that turpentine I smell?"

"It's a new men's cologne," Fletch answered. "Eau Dubuffet. Very big in France at the moment."

"I'd swear it's turpentine."

"I can get you a bottle of it," Fletch said.

"Ach, no, I wouldn't put you to the trouble."

"No trouble," Fletch said. "Honestly."

"Is it expensive stuff?"

"Depends," Fletch said, "on whether you buy it by the ounce or the quart."

"No offence intended," Flynn said, "but I'm not sure I'd want to smell that way. I mean, like a housepainter coming home. Supposed to be manly, is it?"

"Don't you think it is?"

"Well, noses play funny tricks on people. Especially the French."

Grover came back into the living room.

"Inspector, I smell turpentine," he said. "Do you?"

Flynn said, "I do not."

Grover stood in the middle of the room, white at the wrists, wondering how he should settle.

"Do you want me to take the conversation down, Inspector?"

"In truth, I don't want you to take anything down, ever. I have a very peculiar talent, Mister Fletcher. Being a writer-on-art you must have a heightened visual sense. I gather you have a more refined olfactory sense as well, as you pay a fancy price for a French cologne which smells remarkably like turpentine to me. My talent is I never forget a thing I've heard. It's these wonderful Irish ears." The green eyes gleamed impishly as the big man pulled up on his own ears. "Ears of the poets."

Grover was in a side chair, his notebook and pen in his lap at the ready.

In his soft voice, Flynn said, "Grover gave me quite a scolding last night, Mister Fletcher, on the drive home. For not arresting you, you understand. He's convinced we have enough evidence to make a case."

"You're not?" Fletch asked.

"We have evidence," Flynn said, "which is getting thicker by the minute. I explained to Grover I'd rather leave a man his own head and follow him. It's easier to get to know a man when he's free and following his own nature than it is when he's all scrunched up and defensive with his lawyers in a jail cell. A terrible scolding I had. And then this morning you slip our tail, all quite innocently, of course, and fritter away the day doing we know not what."

Fletch did not accept the invitation to report his day.

"In the meantime," he said, "aren't you afraid I might murder someone else?"

"Exactly!" blurted Grover from the side of the room.

Flynn's look told Grover he was a necessary evil.

Softly, Flynn said, "It's my argument that Irwin Maurice Fletcher, even alias Peter Fletcher, would not murder a gorgeous

36

girl in a closed apartment—at least not sober—and then routinely, almost professionally, call the police on himself. He could have wiped things clean, repacked his suitcases, gone back to the airport, and been out of the country in the twitch of a rabbit's nose."

"Thank you," said Fletch.

"Even better," Flynn continued his argument with the side of the room, "he could have dressed the body, taken her down the back stairs in the dark of the night, and left her anywhere in the City of Boston. It wouldn't have disturbed his plans at all."

Fletch had thought about that.

"Instead, what does our boyo do? He calls the police. He doesn't precisely turn himself in, but he does call the police. He deserves some credit, Grover, for his remarkable and demonstrated faith in the institution of the public police."

Grover's ears were red. For a single, impetuous word in argument with his superior he was receiving a considerable chewing out.

"However," said Flynn in a more relaxed manner, "evidence developed today adds considerable weight to Grover's argument. Are you interested in it at all, Mister Fletcher?"

"Of course."

"First of all, what's your understanding as to when Mister Connors went to Italy?"

"I don't know," Fletch answered. "He had occupancy of the villa as of last Sunday."

"And this is Wednesday," Flynn said. "Mrs. Sawyer confirms that Connors was here with her on Saturday, and that he asked her to come in Monday night for a few hours and do a special clean-up because of your arrival Tuesday, yesterday. She did so. Therefore, wouldn't it be natural to assume Connors left for Italy sometime between Saturday night and Monday night?"

Fletch said, "I guess so."

"To this point, we have not been able to establish that he actually did so," Flynn said. "A check of the airlines turned up no transatlantic reservations in the name of Bartholomew Connors."

"He could have flown from New York."

"He didn't," Flynn said. "And as Mister Connors is a partner in an important Boston law firm, I can't believe he would travel under a false passport, unless there is something extraordinary going on here at which we can't even guess."

Fletch said, "I suppose I could call the villa in Italy and see if he's there."

"We may come to that," said Flynn, "But let's not roust the quail until its feathers are wet."

"What?"

"Next we come to Mrs. Sawyer. A widow lady with two grown daughters. One teaches school in Mattapan. She does not live with her mother. The other is in medical school in Oregon. Mrs. Sawyer confirms she has a key to this apartment, but that no one had access to it other than herself. She spent Sunday with a gentleman friend, who is a sixty-year-old divorced accountant, visiting his grandchildren in New Bedford."

Fletch said, "Would you believe I never did suspect Mrs. Sawyer?"

"She had a key," Flynn answered. "Never can tell what bad man might have been taking advantage of her, for reasons of his own. She says that six months ago Connors suffered a particularly—I might even say, peculiarly—painful separation from his wife. There will be a divorce, she says, and I don't doubt it. She says there have been one or more women in this apartment since the separation. She finds their belongings around when she comes to clean. As clothes have never been left, in closets and drawers, she believes she can say no woman has actually lived here since the separation. It substantiates her belief that there has been 'a parade of women through here'. It also substantiates her belief that none of them was ever given, or had, a key."

Grover sneezed.

"As there appear to be paintings in this apartment of great value—is that not right, Mister Fletcher?—we may suppose even further towards certainty that Mister Connors did not dispense keys to this apartment like jelly beans."

"Great value," said Fletch. "Very great value."

He had not toured the paintings to his satisfaction yet, but he had seen enough to be impressed. Besides the Brown in the den, there was a Matisse in the bedroom, a Klee in the living room (on the wall behind Grover), and a Warhol in the dining room.

"The last thing to say about access to the apartment is that there is a back door, in the kitchen. The rubbish goes out that way. There is no key to it. It is twice bolted from the inside. Mrs. Sawyer tells us she is most faithful about bolting it. In fact, when we arrived last night, both bolts were in place. No one could have gone out that way."

"But someone could have come in that way," said Fletch, "bolted the door behind him and gone out the front way."

"Absolutely right," said Flynn. "But how would they, without having known the back door was unbolted?"

"By chance," said Fletch.

"Aye. By chance." Clearly Flynn did not think much of chance.

"Now we come to you," said Flynn.

Grover sat up and clicked his ballpoint pen.

"Washington was good enough to send us both your photograph and your fingerprints." Flynn smiled kindly at Fletch. "Ach, a man has no privacy, anymore."

The kindly smile increased Fletch's discomfort.

"A man is many things," said Flynn. "A bad cheque charge. Two contempt of court charges. Non-payment-of-alimony charges longer than most people's family trees. . . ."

"Get off it, Flynn."

". . . All charges dropped. I do not mean to act as your lawyer," said Flynn, "although I seem to be doing a lot of that. May I recommend that as all these charges were mysteriously dropped, you do something to get them off your record? They're not supposed to be there. And you never know when an official, such as myself, might come along and view them with extreme prejudice. On the principle, you know, that where there's a hatrack there's a hat."

"Thanks for your advice."

"I see you also won the Bronze Star. What the notation 'not delivered' means after the item, I can't guess."

Grover looked around at Fletch with a drill sergeant's disdain.

Flynn said, "You're a pretty dodgy fellow, Irwin Maurice Fletcher."

Fletch said, "I bet you wouldn't even want your daughter to marry me."

"I would resist it," Flynn said, "under the prevailing circumstances."

"You guys don't even like my cologne."

"None of the gentlemen who drive the taxis in from the airport have identified you so far."

"Why do you care about that?"

"We'd like to know if you came in from the airport alone, or with a young lady."

"I see."

"Even the driver who delivered someone from the airport to 152 Beacon Street yesterday afternoon can't identify you. Nor is his record clear on whether he was carrying one passenger or two."

"Terrific."

"Those fellows who work the airport are an independent lot. Fearful independent. And four taxis went from this area last night to the Café Budapest. None of the drivers can identify you or say whether you were alone or not."

"I'm greatly indebted to them all."

"Not everyone is as co-operative as you, Mister Fletcher."

"The bastards."

"Nor did the waiters at the Café Budapest recognize you at all. For a man who wears such an expensive cologne, the fact that you spend an hour or two in a fashionable restaurant and have no one—not even the waiters—recognize you the next day must cut."

"It slashes," said Fletch. "It slashes."

"You'd think waiters would remember a man eating alone, taking up a whole table, even for two, all by himself, wouldn't you? It affects their income."

It was ten minutes to eight.

"That we discovered with your photograph. From your fingerprints we also found out some interesting things."

"I can hardly wait."

"You touched two things in this room—middle-A on the piano keyboard, with your right index finger. I had no idea you are musical."

"I'm not."

"Did I say two things in this room other than the light switches? I meant to. I would guess when you first came into this apartment and were looking around, you turned on the wall switch in the living room, went to the piano, hit middle A, went into the dining room and then the kitchen, leaving the lights on like a 1970 electric company executive."

"I suppose I did."

"The only other things your fingerprints were on in this room were the whisky bottle and the water decanter."

"That would be right."

"It was a fresh bottle. You opened it."

"Yes."

"Mister Fletcher. The whisky bottle was the murder weapon."

The green eyes watched him intensely. Fletch felt them in his stomach. To his side he had the impression of Grover's white face, watching him.

"There were no other fingerprints on the bottle, Mister Fletcher. It had been dusted. Liquor bottles are apt to be dusted while being set out."

"What other fingerprints were in this room?" Fletch asked. "I mean, whose others?"

"Mrs. Sawyer's, the girl's—that is, Ruth Fryer's—and the prints of one other person, a man's, we presume to belong to Bartholomew Connors."

"Were there many of the girl's?"

"A few. Enough to establish she was murdered here. They were the fingerprints of a live person."

Fletch considered his wisdom in saying nothing. At the moment he doubted he could say anything, anyway.

"The disconcerting thing is, Mister Fletcher," continued Flynn with a nerve-shattering gentleness, "that if you remember your laws of physics, the whisky bottle would be a far more reliable, satisfactory, workable murder weapon when it is full and sealed than after it has been uncapped and a quantity has been poured out."

"Oh, my God."

"By opening the whisky bottle and pouring a quantity out, you meant to remove the whisky bottle from suspicion, as the murder weapon."

"It didn't work," said Fletch.

"Ah, that's where my inexperience comes in. A more experienced police officer might have discounted the whisky bottle completely. I remember having to persuade Grover to send it along. It took a few words, didn't it, Grover? Not having come up through the ranks myself, and never having had the benefits of a proper education, I insisted. The boyos in the police laboratory were very surprised the murder weapon was an unbroken, open bottle."

"How do they know it was?"

"Minute traces of hair, skin and blood that match the girl's."

Flynn allowed a long silence. He sat quietly, watching Fletch.

Either he was waiting for Fletch to adjust to this new trauma or he was waiting for Fletch to be indiscreet.

Fletch exercised his right to remain silent.

"Now, Mister Fletcher, would you like to call in a lawyer?"

"No."

"If you think by not calling in a lawyer you're convincing us of your innocence, you're quite wrong."

Grover said, "You're convincing us of your stupidity."

"Now, Grover. Mister Fletcher is not stupid. And now he knows we're not stupid. Maybe he wants to skip the formalities of a lawyer altogether and go ahead with his confession, get the dastardly thing off his chest."

Fletch said, "I know you're not stupid. But I don't know why I'm feeling stupid."

"You look angry."

"I am angry."

"At what?"

"I don't know. I suppose I should have been doing something about this the last twenty-four hours. This murder."

"You haven't been?"

"No."

"Your trust in us has been the most perplexing element in this whole affair," Flynn said. "You're not a naive man."

"You read the record."

"I take it you're not confessing to murder at this point?"

"Of course not."

"He's still not confessing, Grover. Take that down. The man's resistance to self-incrimination is absolutely metallic. Let's go on, then." Flynn sat forward on the divan, elbows on knees, hands folded before him. "You said that night you had never seen Ruth Fryer before in your life."

"Never to my knowledge," answered Fletch.

"With the key number you provided us we went to her hotel, which, by the way, is at the airport. We went through her belongings. We interviewed her room-mate. Then we interviewed her supervisor. Never having seen her before, can you guess what she did for a living?"

"You're not going to say airline stewardess, are you?"

"I am."

"Dandy."

"Trans World Airlines, Mister Fletcher. Temporarily assigned to the job of First Class Ground Hostess at Boston's Logan Airport. On duty to receive passengers aboard Flight 529 from Rome, Tuesday."

"I never saw her! I would remember! She was beautiful!"

Flynn moved back on the divan, possibly in alarm, when Fletch jumped up.

Fletch went up the living room to the piano.

Grover had stood up.

Fletch banged the middle-G major chord.

Then he said, "This has something to do with me."

Flynn said, "What?"

Fletch walked back towards Flynn.

"This murder has something to do with me."

"That's your reaction, is it? Sit down, Grover. Clever man, this Mister Fletcher. It's only taken him twenty-four hours to catch on."

"You've done some wonderful work," said Fletch.

Flynn said, "Oh, my God. Now it's innocent flattery."

"What am I going to do?"

"You might try confessing, you blithering idiot!"

"I would, Inspector, I would." Fletch paced the room. "I still don't think it's personal."

"Now what do you mean by that?"

"I don't think the person who killed Ruth Fryer knows me personally."

"If you're saying you were framed, Mister Fletcher, you've already told us you know no one in town."

"I didn't say I don't know anybody in the world. Lots of people hate me."

"More every minute," said Flynn. "Take Grover there, for example."

"Everybody in Italy knew my plans. Everyone in Cagna, everyone in Rome, everyone in Livorno. The Homeswap people in London. I began making these plans three weeks ago. I wrote old buddies in California saying I would try to get out there while I was in the country. I wrote people in Seattle, Washington."

"All right, Mister Fletcher, we'll put the rest of the world in prison and leave you free."

"But that's not what I'm saying, Inspector. I don't think this is a personal frame. Some sort of an accident happened. I happened to be the next guy in this room after a murder."

"Oh, boyoboyoboy. Like a French philosopher thirty years after he's born he decides he might be involved with the world."

Fletch said, "You guys want to join me for dinner?"

"Dinner! The man's crazy, Grover. As a matter of fact, Mister Fletcher, we were both thinking of asking you to join us."

"I don't care," Fletch said. "Either way. You know the city."

"Well, the truth is," Flynn said to the air, "to this minute the man hasn't acted involved in this case. He's acted as innocent as a reliable witness. He still does. That's the biggest puzzle of all. What are we going to do with him, Grover?"

"Lock him up."

"A very succinct man, this Grover."

"Charge him."

"You know the man can afford to hire fancy lawyers, detectives, make bail, protest all over the press, get postponements, appeal, and appeal all the way to the Supreme Court."

"Lock him up, Frank."

"No." Flynn stood up. "The man didn't leave town yesterday. He didn't leave town today. One may presume he won't leave town tomorrow."

"He'll leave town tomorrow, Inspector."

"Life is simpler this way. We haven't got this man far enough in a corner yet. Although I thought we did."

"What more evidence do we need?"

"I'm not sure. We have pounds of it. I had a hat when I came in. Oh, there it is. It's not polite to talk in front of a man as if he were dead, Grover."

In the hall, Flynn settled the hat on his small head.

"I'm going to get another scolding, Mister Fletcher, I'm sure, all the way home. Maybe Grover can convince me you're guilty. So far you haven't. Good night."

X

A s i t was late (and as Fletch had just discovered he was apparently invisible in a restaurant, anyway) he did not go out to dinner. Tiredly, he searched the kitchen cupboards and came up with a can of hash.

The telephone rang three times while he fed himself.

The first, while he was working the can opener, was a cable from Cagna.

"Connors nice hurt man. Nothing new on father. Much love—Andy."

So Connors was in Italy. Nice, hurt at this moment were irrelevant. He was definitely in Italy.

The second call came before Fletch put the frying pan on to the burner.

"Is this really the hot-shot journalistic wizard, co-agent writer *non pareil*, the great I.M., the one and only, now-you-see-him, now-you-don't Irwin Maurice Fletcher?"

"Jack!" The voice of his old boss, his city editor when he worked in Chicago, Jack Saunders, was too familiar to Fletch ever to confuse with any other voice in the world. For more than a year he had had to listen to that voice, on and off the telephone, for hours at a time. "Where are you?"

"So you've been passing yourself off as Peter Fletcher, eh? I just found an identity-correction advisory from the Boston Police Department on my desk."

"In Chicago?"

"No, sir. Right here in Beantown. You are talking to the night city editor of the *Boston Star*."

"You left the *Post*?"

"If I had realized that murder story involved the great I. M. Fletcher I never would have put it on page seven."

"Page five."

"I would have run it front page with photos linking you and the murdered girl indelibly in the public mind."

"Thanks a lot. So I do know someone in Boston."

"What?"

"How come you left the *Post*?"

"Boston offered more money. Of course, they didn't tell me it costs a lot more to live here in Boston, Taxachusetts. And after you left the *Post*, Fletch, the old place wasn't the same. All the fun went out of it."

"Yeah, sure."

"You made me look real good. Hey, you want a job?"

"Not at the moment. How are Daphne and the kids?"

"Still Daphne and the kids—face powder and peanut butter. Why do you think I work nights?"

Fletch had never known why Jack had remained married. He didn't even like to look at his wife. He considered his kids a big noise.

"Hey, Fletch, they going to indict you?"

"Probably. Who's this Flynn character?"

"You got Frank Flynn? You're in luck. That's why you're not in the slammer already."

"I know."

"They call him Reluctant Flynn. He's very slow to make an arrest. But he's never made a mistake. If he arrests you, boy, you know you've had it."

"What's some b.g. on him?"

"Don't have much. He showed up here in Boston about a year and a half ago, which is very unusual. Cops hardly ever change cities, as you know. I don't even know where he came from. He has the rank of Inspector. Family man. Musical. He plays the violin or something."

"He's good, uh?"

"Cracked about a dozen major cases since he's been here. He's even reopened cases people never expected solved. If you're guilty, he'll get you. By the way, are you guilty?"

"Thanks for asking."

"Free for lunch?"

"When?"

"I was thinking I better get you tomorrow. Visiting people in prisons depresses the hell out of me."

"Working nights you probably want a late lunch, right?"

"About two o'clock. Can you make it?"

"Sure."

"If you have necktie, we can go to Locke-Ober's."

"Where's that?"

"You'll never find it. It's in an alley. Just ask the taxi driver for Locke-Ober's. Want me to spell it?"

"I've got it."

"There are two dining rooms, Fletch. Upstairs and downstairs. I'll meet you downstairs."

"Okay."

"Stay loose, kid. Please don't knock anyone else off without calling the *Star* first. We've got the best photographers in town."

"Bye, Jack."

The third call came while he was eating the hash.

"Fletcher. Darling."

It was Countess de Grassi. The Brazilian Bombshell. Sylvia. Andy's stepmother.

"Hello, Sylvia."

"You didn't return my call, Fletcher."

"What call? Where are you?"

"In Boston, darling. I called earlier and left a message."

"Oh, that Mrs. Sawyer," Fletch said.

He took the message off the desk, crumpled the paper, and threw it hard against a drape.

"I'm at the Ritz-Carlton."

"You can't afford the Ritz-Carlton, Sylvia."

"I'm the Countess de Grassi. You can't expect the Countess de Grassi to stay in, what do you call it, fleabag."

"However, the Ritz-Carlton will expect the Countess de Grassi to pay her bill."

"You're being very unkind, Fletcher. This is none of your business."

"What are you doing here, anyway, Sylvia?"

"What did Angela tell me? You came to Boston to visit your family in Seattle? Even I have a map, Fletcher. I came to visit your family in Seattle, too."

"Sylvia, what I'm doing here doesn't concern you even a little."

"I think yes, Fletcher. You and Angela are, how do you say, pulling some game on me."

"What?"

"You aim to deprive me of what is rightfully mine."

"What are you talking about?"

"First that terrible thing happens to Menti darling, and then you two conspire about me."

"As the grieving widow, aren't you supposed to be in Rome? Or Livorno?"

"You and Angela plan to rob me. Cheat me. Menti would be so mad."

"Nonsense."

"You come over to the hotel right now, Fletcher. Tell me it's not true."

"I can't, Sylvia. I'm miles from the hotel."

"How far? How many miles?"

"Eighteen, twenty miles, Sylvia. Boston's a big city."

"Come in the morning."

"I can't. I'm tied up.

"What does that mean, you're tie-up?'

"I have appointments."

"Lunch, then."

"I have a lunch date."

"Fletcher, I come here to catch you. I'll call the police. They'll listen to the Countess de Grassi at the Ritz-Carlton Hotel."

"I'm sure they would. Sylvia, did Menti ever tell you you're a bitch?"

"You're a son of a bitch, Fletcher."

"That's no way for a Countess to talk."

"I can say worse things in Portuguese and French."

"I've heard them. All right. I'll come to the hotel."

"When?"

"Tomorrow. Late afternoon. Six o'clock."

"Come to my room."

"I will not. I'll meet you in the bar. Six o'clock."

"Six-thirty I call the police if you're not here."

"Don't use their business phone. It upsets them."

"What?"

"Shut up."

The rest of the hash he flushed down the toilet.

X I

''L o o k what some son of a bitch did to my truck!''

Fletch, dressed in jeans, sweater and boots, led the manager of the auto body repair shop through the door.

Now that he knew he was to be followed, Fletch had unbolted the kitchen door and used the back stairs. Actually, the back alley had been a shortcut to the garage on River Street.

He drove the smeared van to the auto body shop feeling as conspicuous as a transvestite at a policemen's ball.

The manager's eyes read "FEED THE PEOPLE". He shook his head slowly.

"Kids."

Hands in his back pockets he walked slowly around to the "ADJUST!" side.

The sun appeared between clouds.

"There's more on the top, too," Fletch said.

48

Coming back, the manager stood on tiptoes and stretched his neck to see the top.

"Have to paint the whole thing."

"Shit," Fletch said.

"Little jerks," the manager said. " 'Feed the people', but screw whoever owns this truck."

"Yeah," Fletch said. "Me."

"You got insurance?"

"Sure."

"Want to check your coverage?"

"Got to have the truck," Fletch said, "whether insurance covers it or not. Can't use it this way."

"What do you do?"

"I'm a plumber," Fletch said.

"Yeah. I guess not too many people would like that truck in their driveways. You might lose a few customers."

"Lose 'em all. Paint it. I'll pay you and knock the insurance company up later myself."

"Same blue?"

"Wouldn't work, would it?"

"Naw. You'd be able to read the black right through it."

"Better paint it black, then."

"Sons of bitches. Even dark red wouldn't work. Even dark green. Ought to have their asses whipped."

"Paint it black."

"You want it black?"

"No, I don't want it black. If I wanted a black truck I would have bought a black truck."

"You'll look like a hearse."

"Friggin' hearse."

"You got the registration?"

"What for?"

"Got to take it into the Registry. Report the change in vehicle colour."

"Screw 'em."

"What?"

"Look." Fletch laid on anger. "I'm the victim of a crime. If the fuzz were doin' what they're supposed to be doin', instead of makin' us fill out papers all the time, my truck wouldn't have been vandalized."

"Sounds reasonable."

"Let 'em go screw. I'll notify 'em when I'm good and ready."

"You want it black, uh?"

"No. But it's gonna be black."

"When do you need it?"

"Right now. I'm late for work right now."

"You can't have the truck today. No way. Tomorrow morning."

"Okay. If that's the best you can do."

"You goin' to go into the Registry?"

"I'm goin' to work. I'll go into the Registry when I get damned good and ready."

"Okay. I understand. We'll paint the truck. You go into the Registry."

"Damned kids," Fletch said. "Weirdos."

"If you get picked up, just don't say where you got the truck painted."

Fletch said, "Screw 'em."

XII

FLETCH listened to the old elevator creak and clank as it climbed to the sixth floor.

The door to apartment 6A opened. A miniature poodle preceded a woman on a leash. It was immediately obvious the woman was tipsy at one-thirty in the afternoon. While Fletch held the elevator door, she rummaged in her purse for her key. The dog watched Fletch curiously. Apparently satisfied she had her key, the woman slammed the door.

"Watch your step," Fletch said.

The woman tripped anyway.

He pushed the "L" button. They sank slowly.

"You the man taking Bart's apartment?"

"Yes," Fletch said. "Name of Fletcher."

How could the woman not have heard of the murder next door? Some drunk.

Fletch patted the dog.

"When did Bart leave, anyway?"

"Saturday," Fletch said. "Sunday. He's using my house in Italy."

"Oh," the woman said.

Fletch wondered how far she could walk the dog.

"That couldn't be," she said.

"What couldn't be?"

"I saw Bart Tuesday."

"You did?"

"Tuesday night. At the place right up the street. The Bullfinch Pub."

"What time?"

She shrugged. She was tired of the conversation.

"Drink time. Six o'clock."

"Are you sure it was Tuesday?"

"He wore a tweed sports jacket. I knew he hadn't just come from the office. Thought it odd. Pretty girl with him."

"What did she look like?"

"Pretty. Young."

The elevator clunked to a stop.

Fletch opened the door.

"Are you sure of this?" he asked.

Passing him, she said, "I'm in love with Bart."

Thinking, Fletch watched her walk unevenly across the lobby.

He caught up to her at the door. He put his hand on the knob to open it.

"Did you speak to Bart Tuesday night?"

"No," she said. "I hate the son of a bitch."

He trailed her through the door.

"That's a nice dog you have there."

"Oh, that's my love. Mignon. Aren't you, Mignon?"

On the sidewalk she extended a gloved hand to Fletch.

"I'm Joan Winslow," she said. "You must come by sometime. For a drink."

"Thank you," Fletch said. "I will."

XIII

THE arrogance of the press," Fletch said, standing to shake hands.

It was two-fifteen. Knowing full well Jack Saunders would

be late, Fletch had ordered and sipped a vodka martini. Through the window he had watched the plainclothesman standing in the alley. A day of quickly travelling clouds, sunlight switched on and off in the alley as if someone were taking time exposures of the discomfited cop. There had been no place for him to park his car. Through the dark window glass of Locke-Ober's the man he was supposed to be watching was sitting at a white-clothed table, sipping a martini, watching him. Fletch had toyed with the idea of inviting him in for a drink.

Jack Saunders said, "Sorry to be a little late. The wife got her eyelashes stuck in the freezer door."

Sitting down, Fletch said, "A reporter is always late because he knows there is no story until he gets there. Still drink gin?"

Jack ordered a martini.

He had not changed much—only more so: his glasses were a little thicker, his sandy hair a little thinner. His belly had let out more than his belt.

"Olde times," Jack said in toast. "With an 'e'."

"To the end of the world," said Fletch. "It will make a hell of a story."

They talked about Jack's new job, where he was living now, their time together on the *Chicago Post*. They had a second drink.

"God, that was funny," Jack was saying. "The time you busted the head of the Internal Revenue Service in Chicago. The Infernal Revenue Service. The guy was as guilty as hell. They had him in court. They couldn't get the evidence on him because his wife had all the evidence, and they couldn't call her to testify because she was his wife, even though they were separated."

"The newspaper was being very polite about it," Fletch said, "following the court in its frustration, as the man Flynn might say."

"Journalistic responsibility, Fletch. Journalistic responsibility. Will you never learn?"

"Sloppy legwork," Fletch said. "I didn't do anything any junior-grade F.B.I. man couldn't have done."

"What did you do, anyway?"

"I can't tell you."

"Come on, I'm not your boss any more."

"You might be again one day, though."

"I hope so. Come on, we're not in Illinois, the guy's in jail. . . ."

"Why the hell should I give you ideas? You were reporting the court record as docilely as the rest of the idiot editors."

"Yeah, but when you got the story, I ran it."

"Yes, you did. Of course, you did. I'm supposed to be grateful? You won a prize and then made a bloody long speech about team efforts."

"I let you hold the prize. Ten or fifteen minutes. I remember handing it to you."

"And I remember your taking it back."

"You're ashamed. You're ashamed of what you did."

"I got the story."

"You're ashamed of how you got it. That's why you won't tell me."

"I'm a little ashamed."

"How did you do it?"

"I poured sugar in the wife's gas tank and followed her home. When her engine died I stopped to help her. Did the whole bit, fiddled under her hood, pretended to adjust things, told her to try it again."

"That's funny."

"Drove her home. It was eight o'clock at night. She offered me a drink."

"You entrapped her."

"Is that the word? The friendship ripened. . . ."

"How was she in bed?"

"Sort of cold."

"Jeez, you'd do anything for a story."

"She had her good points. They weren't far from her chin."

"I'm sure you told her you were a member of the press."

"I think I told her I sold air-conditioning units. I don't know how the idea occurred to me. Something about the cool breezes from her every orifice."

"But you plugged her in." Jack's eyes were wet from laughing. "And plugged her in. And plugged her in. And plugged her in."

"Look, the lady was blackmailing her husband and therefore he was embezzling from the United States government. The courts couldn't get at her because she was still legally his wife. What did she deserve?"

"Yeah, but I still don't know how you did it."

"Well, we took a vacation together. In Nevada. The dear thing was divorced before she knew it."

"I remember the expense account. Oh, boy, do I remember

53

the expense account. The Accounting Department did a dance all over my ass. With hiking boots. You mean the *Chicago Post* paid for somebody's divorce?"

"Actually, yes. Well, it freed her as a witness."

"Oh, that's funny. If they only knew."

"I listed it properly—legal fees incurred while travelling."

"Jeez, we thought you got busted for pot or something. Maybe got caught with your pants down in a casino...."

"Don't ask. I told the lady we had to go back to Chicago to get married. Had to get my birth certificate, that sort of thing, you know."

"You actually told her you were going to marry her?"

"Of course. Why else would she get a divorce? I mean, under those circumstances?"

"You are a bastard."

"So my father said. Anyway, once the lady realized she was divorced and about to land at O'Hare International Airport in Chicago, she panicked. She envisioned all sorts of men in blue suits waiting for her when she got off the plane. So I convinced her the best thing to do was to give me the evidence, pack her bags, and split immediately."

"Which she did?"

"Which she did. All the evidence, plus a signed deposition, all of which, you may remember, we published."

"We certainly did."

"I told her I'd meet her in Acapulco as soon as I found my birth certificate."

"What happened to her?"

"I never heard. As far as I know, she's still waiting in Acapulco."

"Oh, you're a terrible man. You're a son of a bitch. You're a shit, Fletcher. But you're funny."

"It was a pretty good story," Fletch said. "Shall we eat?"

They dug into their Châteaubriand.

"Did you see the *Star* this morning?" Jack asked.

"No. Sorry."

"We gave more space to your story this morning. Ran a picture of the girl."

"Thanks."

"Had to. Pretty damning evidence they've got on you, Fletch. Your fingerprints were on the murder weapon."

"The police gave you that?"

"Yup."

"Trying to build a public case against me. The bastards."

"Poor Fletch. As if you never did such a thing yourself. What's the next development to expect?"

"My confession. But don't hold your breath."

"I figure if Flynn hasn't arrested you, he's got a reason."

"If you look through the window to your right, you'll see my flat-footed escort."

"Oh, yeah. Even paranoids have enemies, I've heard."

"Actually, I think I've got the case cracked. It was an impersonal, coincidental frame."

"So, who did it?"

"One of two people. Rather not go into it now."

"You always did play stories close to the chest. Until you had them on paper."

"Twists and turns, Jack. Twists and turns. Every story has its twists and turns. By the way, do you think you'd let me use your library? There are some people I'd like to look up."

"Sure. Who?"

"This guy, Bart Connors, for one. I'm using his apartment."

"Don't know much about him. Partner in one of those State Street law firms. He's taxation or something."

"Maybe I could come in some afternoon, while you're there."

"You bet. Mondays and Tuesdays I take off. You'll probably want to come sooner than that."

"Yeah. God knows where I'll be next Monday."

"I've been to Norfolk Prison," said Jack. "It's not bad, as prisons go. Clean. Got a good shop. Over-crowded, of course."

"Maybe that's why Flynn hasn't arrested me."

"I don't think you should come into the office using the name Fletcher, though. The publisher might resent a murder suspect going through our files."

"Okay. What name should I use?"

"Smith?"

"That's a good one."

"Jones? I've got it—Brown."

"Has a nice ring to it."

"I'm not as inventive as you are, Fletch."

"How about Jasper dePew Mandeville the Fourth?"

"That's a good one. Very convincing."

"I'll use the name Locke."

"John?"

"Ralph."

"Ralph!"

"Somebody's got to be called Ralph."

They both had their coffee black.

Jack said, "For some reason, I've hesitated to ask you what you're doing these days. I guess I'm afraid what you might tell me."

"I've gone back to writing about art."

"Oh, yeah. You were doing that in Seattle. Not quite as exciting as investigative reporting."

"It has its moments."

"How can you afford it? I mean, you're not writing for anyone, right?"

"An uncle left me some money."

"I see. I. M. Fletcher finally ripped somebody off. Always knew you would."

"Did the de Grassi story come over the wires?"

"De Grassi?"

"From Italy. Count Clementi de Grassi."

"Oh, yeah. That's a weird one. I don't think we used it. What was the story? He was kidnapped, and then when the ransom wasn't paid, he was murdered, right?"

"Right. I expect to marry his daughter, Angela."

"Oh. Why didn't they pay the ransom?"

"They didn't have the money. Nothing like it."

"A great tragedy."

"There's only the young wife, the present Countess de Grassi, about forty, and Angela, who is in her early twenties. They haven't got a dime. Ransom was over four million dollars."

"Then why was he kidnapped?"

"Somebody got the wrong de Grassi family. They have the title, you know, a falling-down palace outside Livorno, and they keep a small apartment at a good address in Rome."

"Pretty horrible story. Maybe we should have run it."

"I don't think so," said Fletch. "It's far away, has nothing to do with Boston. No use in advertising crime."

Jack Saunders paid the bill.

"Nice eating off a newspaper again," Fletch said. "As a kindness, I guess I should go get that cop off his flat feet. For him, I'll take a taxi home. Otherwise, I would walk."

"Congratulations," Jack said. "I mean, about getting married."

Fletch said, "This is the real thing."

XIV

I T W O U L D be nine-thirty at night in Cagna, Italy.

Fletch wandered around the apartment, with his coat and tie off. He toured the paintings.

He had evidence, from an unreliable witness, Joan Winslow from apartment 6A, that Bart Connors had been in Boston the night of the murder. Tuesday night. No, he had more than that. Flynn had said there was no evidence from the airlines Connors had flown out of the country anytime between his being seen by Mrs. Sawyer on Saturday night and Tuesday night. Yet yesterday, Wednesday, Andy had seen him in Cagna.

Should he tell Flynn what the woman in 6A had said?

Fletch had worked with the police before. With them, against them, around them. Flynn was pretty good, but it was Fletch's freedom Fletch was fighting for. So far, he had been entirely too trusting.

He'd roust the quail whether its feathers were wet or not.

Fletch checked his watch again, and placed a call to his villa in Cagna.

"Hello?"

"Andy?"

"Fletch!"

"What are you doing in Cagna?"

"You asked me to come up."

"That was yesterday."

"Why did you call here, Fletch?"

"Did you spend the night?"

"Oh, I had car trouble."

"The Porsche?"

"Bart said it was the diaphragm or something."

" 'Bart said!' This is the second night, Andy."

"Yes. The car will be ready in the morning."

"Andy!"

"Wait until I turn the record player down, Fletch. I can't hear too well."

She came back in a few seconds and said, "Hello, Fletch, darling."

"Andy, what are you doing spending the night at my house with Bart Connors?"

"That has no business for you, Fletcher. Just because I marry you has nothing to do with where I spend last night."

"Listen to me, will you? Is Bart Connors there?"

Andy hesitated. "Of course."

"Then get out of that house. Sneak out and run down to the hotel or something."

"But, darling, why?"

"There is some evidence your host has a terrible temper."

"Temper? Nonsense. He's a kitten."

"Will you do as I say?"

"I don't think so. We're just beginning dinner."

"I think you'd better come here, Andy. To Boston."

"I have to go back to Rome. See what the grand Countess is doing."

"The Countess is here."

"Where?"

"In Boston. Sylvia is here."

"The bitch."

"Why don't you fly from Genoa?"

"I can't believe you, Fletch. This is something you're putting on. For jealousy. I'm not jealous of the people you spend time with."

"Andy, you're not listening."

"No, and I'm not going to. I don't know why you called here, anyway. I'm supposed to be in Rome."

"To talk to Bart Connors."

"Then talk to him."

"Andy, after I talk to Connors, please come back on the phone."

She said, "I'll get him."

The pause was interminable.

"Hello? Mister Fletcher?"

"Mister Connors? Everything all right at the villa?"

"Your girlfriend dropped in yesterday. She'd lost a necklace here. We put on quite a search for it."

"What's wrong with the car?"

"What car?"

"The Porsche."

"It's quite a long drive to Rome. Isn't it?"

"When did you arrive in Cagna?"

"Yesterday."

"Wednesday?"

"Yes, that's right."

"I thought you were going out on Sunday."

"My plans got mixed up. The person I thought was coming with me couldn't make it."

"You waited for her?"

"My powers of persuasion were not adequate to the task. Good thing I didn't become a trial lawyer."

"You flew through New York?"

"Montreal."

"Why Montreal? Is that better?"

"I had a late business dinner there. It's very nice of you to call, Mister Fletcher, but it's sort of expensive for a chat. I hope you called collect—on your phone."

"And Ruth said she wouldn't go with you?"

"What?"

"Ruth. She said she wouldn't go with you to Cagna?"

"Who's Ruth?"

"The girl you were trying to take to Cagna with you."

"I don't understand you, Mister Fletcher."

"Mister Connors, I think you had better think of coming back to Boston."

"What?"

"A young woman was murdered in your apartment. Tuesday night. I found the body."

"What are you talking about?"

"Her name was Ruth Fryer."

"I don't know anyone named Ruth Prior."

"Fryer. She was hit over the head with a whisky bottle."

"Am I crazy, or am I just not understanding you?"

"A girl named Ruth Fryer was killed in your apartment Tuesday night."

"Did you do it?"

"Mister Connors, it appears you are a suspect in a murder case."

"I am not. I'm in Italy."

"You were in Boston at the time of the murder."

"I had nothing to do with it, and I'm going to have nothing to do with it. No one could have gotten into that apartment. You're the only one who has a key."

"And Mrs. Sawyer."

"And Mrs. Sawyer. My key is here. Is this some kind of a joke?"

"You were seen in Boston on Tuesday night, Mister Connors."

"I stayed at the Parker House Monday night. I had already moved out of the apartment and didn't want to mess it up. Look, Fletcher, I don't know what the hell you're saying. Was there any damage to the apartment itself?"

"No."

"I have nothing to do with this. I don't know anyone named Ruth Fryer. And who the hell are you to question me, anyway?"

"Another suspect in the same murder case."

"Well, don't lay it off on me, pal. I'm sorry somebody's dead, and I'm sorry somebody's dead in my apartment, but I don't know anything about it."

"You're a kitten."

"What?"

"Will you let me talk to Andy again?"

"If I came running back, then I would be involved. The newspapers would question me. I'm a lawyer in Boston, Fletcher. I can't afford that. Jesus Christ, did you kill somebody in my apartment?"

"No. I didn't."

"Whom have the police questioned so far?"

"Me."

"Whom else?"

"Me."

"Fletcher, why don't you move out of my apartment?"

"No, I'm not going to do that."

"I'll call the law firm. Somebody's got to protect my interest."

"I thought you didn't have an interest."

"I don't. Jesus. You've ruined dinner. Do you have another bottle of gin somewhere?"

"Yeah. In the lower cupboard in the pantry. It's Swiss."

"This is a terrible thing to happen. I'm staying away from it."

"Okay. Let me talk to Andy."

Connors exhaled into the mouthpiece.

Then the line went dead.

He had hung up.

If Fletch had accomplished nothing else, he had ruined their evening together.

"Pan American Airways. Miss Fletcher speaking."
   "What?"
"Pan American Airways. Miss Fletcher speaking."
   "Your name is Fletcher?"
   "Yes, sir."
   "This is Ralph Locke."
   "Yes, Mister Locke."
   "Miss Fletcher, I'd like to fly from Montreal to Genoa, Italy, late Tuesday night. Is that possible?"
   "One moment, sir, I'll check." It was scarcely a moment. "TWA's Flight 805 leaves Montreal at eleven p.m. Tuesday evening, with a connection in Paris for Genoa, Italy."
   "What's your first name?"
   "Linda, sir."
   "Linda Fletcher? You weren't ever married to someone named Irwin Maurice Fletcher, were you?"
   "No, sir."
   "You didn't sound familiar. How long does it take to fly to Montreal from Boston?"
   "About forty minutes, actual flying time, sir. Eastern has a flight at eight p.m., which would give you plenty of time."
   "Is there a later flight?"
   "Delta flies to Montreal at nine-thirty p.m. That would still give you plenty of time."
   Talking to her, as obviously she was pushing buttons on a computer console, was like talking to someone in space. A short delay preceded her every answer.
   "Should I make these reservations for you, Mister Locke?"
   "Perhaps later. I'll call back. Where are you from, Miss Fletcher?"
   "Columbus, Ohio, sir."
   "Ohio's a nice place," Fletch said. "I've never been there."

Fletch shaved, showered and put on a fresh shirt. It was almost six o'clock.
   At six-thirty the Countess was going to call the police on him if he didn't meet her in the Ritz bar.
   Instead, the police called him.
   Necktie over his shoulders, he answered the bedroom phone.

"How are you today, Mister Fletcher?"

"Ah, Flynn. I wanted to talk to you."

"Did you want to confess, by any chance?"

"No, that wasn't what I was thinking."

"Sorry if I appear to be ignoring you, but a City Council-woman was murdered in her bath this morning and since it's a politically sensitive case, I've been assigned to it. I've never held with taking baths in the morning, anyway, but when you're in politics God knows how many baths a day you need."

"What was she killed with?"

"The murder weapon? An ice pick, Mister Fletcher."

"Messy."

"Aye, it was that. She took the first thrust in the throat, which seems peculiarly appropriate. I mean, it makes it seem far more the political crime, doesn't it?"

"I wouldn't like your job, Flynn."

"It has its downs. She was a chubby old thing."

"Inspector, I've discovered a few things which might be of interest to you."

"Have you, indeed?"

"The woman in the next apartment, 6A, name Joan Winslow, says she saw Bart Connors in Boston Tuesday night, at about six o'clock, having a drink up the street at the Bullfinch Pub with an attractive young woman."

"Now, that's interesting. We'll talk with her."

"I suspect she's not too reliable a witness. But I've talked with Bart Connors in Italy."

"Have you? And now that you've talked with him, will he stay in Italy?"

"Apparently. He refuses to come back."

"Small wonder. It's not his coming this direction I worry about. We have an extradition agreement with Italy, whereas we don't with one or two other countries he might find attractive."

"He says he flew to Genoa through Montreal late Tuesday night."

"We know. The nine-thirty Delta Flight 770 to Montreal; the eleven o'clock Trans World Airlines Flight 805 to Paris."

"He had plenty of time to do murder here."

"Yes, he did."

"But the important thing is that he said the reason for his delay in departure, by two or three days, was that he was trying to talk a girl, a specific girl, into going to Italy with him."

"But Ruth Fryer wasn't in Boston until Monday night."

"He may have been waiting for her."

"He may have been."

"Bought her a drink up the street, brought her back here for further persuasion, lost his temper, and bashed her."

"It sounds very reasonable."

"I would guess he's been through a tough time emotionally lately."

"There's no way of knowin' that. Every time I've made guesses as to what goes on between a married couple, I've been wrong. Even when they're divorcing."

"Anyway. . . ."

"At least your theories in defence of yourself are becoming fuller. More cogent, if you know what I mean. I'm pleased to see, for example, you're beginning to accept the idea that someone else hit Ruth Fryer over the head with a bottle—not that she bopped herself and put the bottle back carefully on the tray across the room before expiring."

"You'll talk to the Winslow woman?"

"We will. In the meantime, we have the autopsy report on the Fryer girl. She was killed between eight and nine o'clock Tuesday night."

"The airport is ten minutes away. Connors' flight was at nine-thirty."

"It is ten minutes away. When the Boston police are succeeding at their traffic duty. She had had about three drinks of alcohol in the preceding three or four hours."

"At the Bullfinch Pub."

"That can't be determined. Despite her naked condition, she had not had sexual relations with a male in the preceding twenty-four hours."

"Of course not. She refused him."

"Mister Fletcher, would a man of Mister Connors' age and experience, in this advanced age, murder a girl because she refused his sexual advances?"

"Certainly. As you said, if he'd had enough to drink."

"I would think, even with liquor he'd have to have a deep-seated psychological problem to do in a young lady who said 'No'."

"How do we know he hasn't?"

"I'll grant you, Mister Fletcher, there is some evidence against your landlord. And, under the circumstances, I don't even perceive your trying to pin it on him as being particularly ignoble."

"I have the advantage, Flynn. I know I'm not the murderer. I'm trying to find out who is."

"However, the evidence against yourself is a great deal stronger. Ruth Fryer was the Ground Hostess for First Class passengers of Trans World Airlines Flight 529 from Rome Tuesday. Your Ground Hostess. Several hours later, after having been dressed for the evening, she's found murdered in your apartment. Your fingerprints were on the murder weapon."

"Okay, Flynn. What can I say?"

"You can confess, Mister Fletcher, and let me get on with the City Councilwoman's murder."

"Person, Inspector."

"What's that?"

"Councilperson. City Councilperson."

"Fat lot of good the distinction will do her now she's been slain in the tub. Will you confess, lad?"

"Of course not."

"Do you still think the murder's an accidental and impersonal coincidence? Is that still your lame stand?"

"Yes."

"Grover's of the fixed opinion we should arrest you and charge you with murder before you do harm to someone else."

"But you're not going to."

"I'm inclining very much that way."

"Did you ever find that girl who gave me directions in that square Tuesday night? The square with the Citgo sign?"

"Of course not. We haven't even looked. We'd have to interview the entire female population at Boston University, and that still wouldn't cover all the young women who might be in Kenmore Square at that time of night. There are night clubs there."

"Oh."

"It's no good, lad. The evidence is piled up. I doubt we'll ever get more."

"I hope not."

"It's not precisely warm of me to ask you to confess by telephone, but there is this other murder."

"Will you stop giving the evidence you have to the newspapers? You're convicting me."

"Ach, that. Well, that puts as much pressure on me as it does on you."

"Not quite, Inspector. Not quite."

"Well, I'll leave it alone for a while. Give you time to think. Get a lawyer. I have a natural instinct to not do precisely what Grover tells me to do. You might even get a psychiatrist."

"Why a psychiatrist?"

"It's your seeming innocence that puzzles me. I sincerely believe you think you didn't kill Ruth Fryer. The evidence says you did."

"You mean you think I blacked it out."

"It's been known to happen. The human mind plays amazing tricks. Or am I doing the wrong thing in giving you a line of legal defence?"

"I guess anything's possible."

"The thing is, Mister Fletcher, what I'm saying is, you have to keep an open mind to the evidence. Even you. You might start to begin to believe the evidence. You see, we have to believe the evidence."

"There's a lot of evidence."

"I shouldn't be doing this on the phone. But there's this other body."

"I understand."

"I suppose we could work a thing whereby the court appoints a psychiatrist for you. . . ."

"Not yet, Flynn."

"Do you agree this interpretation of the crime and its solution is a possibility?"

"Yes. Of course."

"Good lad."

"But it didn't happen."

"I'm sure you don't think so."

"I know so."

"That, too. Well, that's my best guess at the moment. Got to get back to my chubby City Councilperson."

"Inspector?"

"Yes?"

"I'm about to go to the Ritz-Carlton."

"Yes?"

"Just warning you. You'd better have your men keep a pretty sharp eye on the side door this time."

"They will, Mister Fletcher. They will."

XV

FLETCH walked the "eighteen, twenty miles" to the Ritz-Carlton, which was around a corner and up a few blocks.

He hung around the lobby, looking at the books on the newsstand, until his watch said six-thirty-five.

Then he went into the bar.

Countess Sylvia de Grassi was receiving considerable attention from the waiters. Her drink was finished, but one was dusting the clean table, another was bringing her a fresh plate of olive hors d'oeuvres, a third was standing by, admiring her with big eyes.

Sylvia, near forty, had brightly tousled bleached hair, magnificent facial features, smooth skin, and apparently the deepest cleavage ever spotted in Boston. Her dress was cut not to cover her breasts but to suggest the considerable structural support needed. Clearly there was nothing holding them down. They preceded her like an offering.

"Ah, Sylvia. Nice trip?"

He kissed her cheek as a socially acceptable alternative.

"Sorry to be a little late." All three waiters held his chair. "Mrs. Sawyer got her eyelashes caught in the freezer door."

"What's this, Mrs. Sawyer—freezer door?"

Sylvia's big brown eyes were puckered with impatient suspicion.

"Just the best excuse I've heard all day."

"Now, Flesh, I am not going to have any of your double-talk in English. I want the truth."

"Absolutely. What are you drinking?"

"Campari in soda."

"Still watching your figure, uh? Might as well. Everyone else is." He said to all the waiters—as he could get the eye of none of them—"A Campari and soda and a Bath Towel. You don't have a Bath Towel? Then I'll just have a Chivas and water. Now, Sylvia, you were saying you were about to tell the truth. Why are you in Boston?"

"I come to Boston to stop you. You and Angela. I know you conspire against me. You plan to rob my paintings."

"Nonsense, dear lady. What makes you think a thing like that?"

"Because. In Angela's room I found your notes. Your address, 152 Beacon Street, Boston. Your telephone number. Also a list of the paintings."

66

"I see. From that you reasonably concluded I came to Boston to find the paintings."

"I know you did."

"And you followed me."

"I come ahead of you. I fly Rome, New York, then Boston. I wanted to be waiting when you got off the airplane in Boston. I wanted you to run right into me."

"What fun. What held you up?"

"I missed the connection in New York."

"You mean, you were here in Boston on Tuesday?"

"I was. Five o'clock I arrived Boston."

"My, my. And all that time I thought I knew no one in Boston. What did you do then?"

"I came here to the hotel. I call you. No answer."

"I went out to dinner."

"I call you next day, yesterday, leave a message. You never called back."

"Okay, so you killed Ruth Fryer."

"What you say? I kill no one."

She retracted her supercarriage while the waiter served her drink.

"What's this talk of kill?"

Fletch ignored the drink in front of him.

"Sylvia, I don't have the paintings. I've never seen the paintings. I don't know where the paintings are. I'm not even sure I've got the story about the paintings straight."

"Then why are you in Boston with a list of the paintings? Tell me that."

"I'm in Boston to do research on a book about an American painter named Edgar Arthur Tharp, Junior. I brought a list of the mythical de Grassi paintings with me, just in case I ran across any reference to them. Boston's a centre of culture."

"How do the Americans say it? Bullshit, Flesh! You're engaged to marry my daughter, Angela. The day after her father's funeral, you jump on a plane with the list of the missing paintings in your pocket, and come to Boston, U.S. America. What else to think?"

"Stepdaughter. Angela is your stepdaughter."

"I know. She is not mine. She plans to rob me."

"Has Menti's will been read?"

"No. Bullshit lawyers will not read it. They say, too much confusion. Police say, this matter settled, go away, Countess, cry.

67

Bullshit lawyers say this matter not settled. So Countess go away and cry some more. All this time, Angela, you rob, rob, rob me."

"Angela's mentioned the paintings. Menti mentioned the paintings. You talk about the paintings. I've never seen the paintings. I don't even know they ever existed."

"They exist! I've seen them! They are my paintings, now that Menti is dead. Poor Menti. They are what I have in the world. He left them to me."

"You don't know that. The will hasn't been read. They're the de Grassi paintings. He might have left them to his daughter, who is a de Grassi. He might have left them to both of you. Do you know what Italian estate laws are concerning such matters? They might not even be mentioned in the will. They've been gone a long time. He might have left them all to a museum in Livorno, or Rome."

"Nonsense! Menti would never do that to me. Menti loved me. It was his great sadness that we had the paintings no more. He knew how I loved those paintings."

"I'm sure you did. So what makes you think the paintings are in Boston?"

"Because you come here. The day after the funeral. You and Angela have your heads together. Angela wants those paintings. She's going to rob me!"

"Okay, Sylvia. I give up. Tell me about the paintings."

"The de Grassi Collection. Nineteen paintings. Some, Menti had from his parents, others he collected himself. Before World War Two."

"And I suspect during and after World War Two."

"Before, during, after World War Two."

"He was an Italian officer during the war?"

"He did nothing about the war. The de Grassis turned their palace, Livorno, into a hospital."

"Palace? Big old house."

"They took care of Italian soldiers, citizens, German soldiers, American soldiers, British soldiers—everybody soldiers. Menti told me. He spent his fortune. He hired doctors, nurses."

"And picked up a few paintings."

"He had the paintings. Them he did not sell. Even years after the war. Angela was born. He sold his land, bit by bit, the de Grassi land, but never sold a painting. You know what the paintings are. You have the list."

"Yeah. From what I've been able to find out so far, they've never been recorded. Anywhere. No one knows they exist."

"Because they have always been in a private collection. The de Grassi Collection. See? You are looking for them!"

Fletch said, "I made an inquiry."

"You son of a bitch! You are looking for them. You lie to me!"

"Andy gave me the list. I said I would make an inquiry. I've asked one dealer about one painting. Please don't call me a son of a bitch anymore. I'm sensitive."

"You and Angela are not going to rob me of my paintings!"

"You've made that point pretty well, too. You're accusing me of robbery. Go on with the story. When were the paintings stolen?"

"Two years ago. Stolen overnight. Every one of them."

"From the house in Livorno?"

"Yes."

"Weren't the servants there?"

"Ah, they're no good. Very old, very sleepy. Deaf and blind. Ria and Pep. Menti had great loyalty for them. Last two de Grassi servants. I told him they stupid old fools. Never should he leave such a fortune in paintings to their charge."

"They heard nothing and saw nothing?"

"Flesh, they didn't even realize they were gone until we came back to the house and said, 'Where are the paintings?' They were so used to them. They had seen them all their lives. They didn't even recognize when they were gone. All the time we were away, they never even went into the front of the house!"

"And the paintings weren't insured?"

"Never. Stupid old Italian counts do not insure things they've always had, always been used to."

"Menti was a stupid old Italian count, eh?"

"About insurance, he was as bad as the rest of them. As bad as the Catholic Church."

"He probably couldn't afford the premiums."

"He couldn't afford the premiums. Then, whoosh, one day they were gone. The police did not care so much. Just some paintings, they said. There was no big insurance company making them find the paintings and kill the people who stole them."

"You weren't in Livorno when the paintings were stolen?"

"Menti and I were on our honeymoon. In Austria."

"That's not far." Fletch tried one of the olives. "So where are the paintings, Sylvia?"

"What you mean, 'Where are the paintings, Sylvia?'"

"I think you stole them yourself. Is that what you don't want me to find out? Is that why you're here?"

"Stole them myself!"

"Sure. In your mid-thirties, you marry a sixty-seven-year-old Italian count, with a palace in Livorno and an apartment in Rome. You're his third wife. He's your second husband. Your first husband was Brazilian?"

"French." Her face vacillated between studied amusement and murderous rage.

"You have, let's say, international connections. You marry the old boy. You go on your honeymoon. You discover he's broke. Or, he has very little money. Nothing like the fortune you thought he had. You realize his whole fortune is in these paintings. He's thirty years older than you. You think he might leave the paintings to his daughter, to a museum. After all, you told him you married him for love, right? So you arranged to have the paintings stolen. You stashed them away. Did you even arrange to have Menti kidnapped and murdered? Now you're scared to death I'm going to catch you."

The amusement in her face was agonized.

She said, "I hate you."

"Because I'm right."

"I loved Menti. I would do nothing to harm him. I did not steal the paintings."

"But you, too, left Rome the day after the funeral."

"To catch you."

"It's one thing for the prospective son-in-law of the deceased to leave town the day after the funeral. It's something else for the grieving widow to skip."

"If I killed anyone, I would kill you."

"Which brings up another question, Sylvia. Did you come to my apartment Tuesday night? Was the door opened by a naked young lady who said she was waiting for Bart Connors? Not being able to make sense out of her, did you hit her with a bottle of whisky?"

"I not make sense out of you."

"Of course not."

"You say your apartment is twenty miles away. That's what you said."

"It's just around the corner, Sylvia. And you know it."

"I don't know what you're talking about. 'Killing a girl.' First you say I kill Menti, and then you say I kill some girl. You're crazy in the head."

"I've already admitted that possibility today."

"Who is this man you talked to about the paintings?"

"I have to have a few secrets of my own."

Fletch stood and neatly put his chair back under the table. "Thanks for the drink, Sylvia."

"You not paying?"

"You invited me. It's a whole new world, babe. You pay."

XVI

"I GUESS it's a pretty good job," Fletch said. "I can't read the shit through the paint."

"It's a nice job if you like hearses," the manager said. "What will a black truck do for your plumbing business?"

"I don't know," Fletch said. "Might improve it."

"Neighbours will think you're carrying out a body."

Friday morning was cool and cloudy again.

The manager said, "Did you get down to the Registry?"

Fletch said, "I brought cash for you."

"I'll get the bill."

Fletch paid him off and took the keys to his black panel truck.

"Okay, fella," the manager said. "You get stopped in that truck and the registration don't match, don't say where you got it painted."

"I'll get to the Registry tomorrow," Fletch said. "Saturday."

When he was getting into the truck, the manager said, "Don't suppose you got a spare minute?"

"Why? What's the matter?"

"Leak. In the men's room."

"No, thanks," said Fletch. "Don't need to."

XVII

"WILL you tell Mister Saunders that Mister Ralph Locke is in the lobby waiting to see him?"

The smile of the woman at the reception desk was a widow's smile. In her fifties, she had learned to smile again, after a funeral, after someone had given her a job, a new but lesser life. Fletch guessed she was the widow of a journalist—perhaps one of those later names inscribed in a long plaque on the lobby wall, starting with 1898 and dribbling through years of war, collisions with fire trucks, and accidents with demon rum.

"A copy boy will be right down to get you," she smiled.

In mid-afternoon, Fletch had gone down to the Ford Ghia parked at the curb.

There were six parking tickets under the windshield wipers.

Knowing the two men in the car across the street were plain-clothesmen assigned to watch him, he tore the six parking tickets up and dropped the pieces in the street.

They did not arrest him for destruction of public records, contempt, or littering.

So he led them to the *Boston Daily Star* building.

It was a wet, greystone building in the bowels of the city. The narrow streets around it were clogged with *Star* delivery trucks.

Fletch found two places to park.

He drove the Ghia into one.

And waved the policemen into the other.

A copy boy led him through the huge, smelly old city room. Jack Saunders was waiting for him near the copy desk.

Fletch said, "I see the publisher has paid off the mortgage."

Shaking hands, Jack looked around the large, yellow room. A hundred years of nicotine had attached itself to the walls, ceiling and floor.

"I think he's almost got it paid off. Another few payments."

In the morgue, Jack said to the young help behind the counter, "Randy, this is Ralph Locke, *Chicago Post*, here working on a story."

"I know your by-line, Mister Locke," the kid said.

"Ah, shit," said Fletch.

Jack laughed. "Show him around, will you, Randy?"

Fletch knew the alphabet. He also knew left from right.

Very shortly he got rid of the young hyprocrite.

First the regional *Who's Who.*

An item on page 208 read :

Connors, Bartholomew, lawyer; b. Cambridge, Mass. Feb. 7, 1936; s. Ralph and Lilliam (Day) C.; B.A. Dartmouth, 1958; Harvard Law, 1961; m. Lucy Aureal Hyslop, June 6, 1963; Tullin, O'Brien and Corbett, 1962–; partner, 1971. Harvard Club, Boston; Harvard Club, New York. Boylston Club; Trustee, Inst. Modern Art; Director Childes Hospital, Control Systems, Inc., Wardor-Rand, Inc., Medical Implements, Inc. Home : 152 Beacon St., Boston. Office : 32 State St., Boston.

An item on page 506 read :

Horan, Ronald Risom, educator, author, art dealer; b. April 10, 1919, Burlington, Vt.; s. Charles N. and Beatrice (Lamson) H.; B.A. Yale, 1940, U.S. Navy, 1940–45 (Commander); M.A. Cambridge, 1947; Ph.D Harvard, 1949; m. Grace Gulkis, Oct. 12, 1948 (d. 1953). Harvard fac. 1948–; ass't. prof., dept Fine Arts, 1954–. Cont. ed., *Objects*, 1961–65; cont. ed., *Art Standards International*, 1955–. Author, *Themes and Images*, September Press, 1952; *Techniques in Object Authentication*, September Press, 1959. Director, Horan Gallery, 1953–. Lecturer, Cambridge, 1966. Athenaeum, St. Paul's Society, Bosely Club; Advisor, Karkos Museum, 1968–. Home : 60 Newbury St., Boston. Office : Horan Gallery, 60 Newbury St., Boston.

There was no item in *Who's Who* for Inspector Francis Xavier Flynn.

There was little in the newspaper clipping files directly concerning either Connors or Horan.

Connors was represented by a single clipping. Once he had issued to the press and public the recent tax statements of a then-gubernatorial candidate, a client and Harvard Law School classmate, who did not win.

The story referred to Connors as "senior partner of the State Street law firm, Tullin, O'Brien and Corbett and son of former U.S. Ambassador to Australia, Ralph Connors".

Connors' photograph showed a fair-sized, athletic-looking man.

The file on Ambassador Ralph Connors apparently had been cleaned out, except for the obituary. Until becoming Ambassador, he had been Chairman of the Board of Wardor-Rand, Inc. He died in 1951.

There was no photograph of Ronald Risom Horan.

The only news item concerning Horan reported an attempted burglary of the Horan Gallery in 1975. From the way the item was written, Fletch guessed it had been taken straight from a police spokesperson. There was no actual confirmation. There was no follow-up story.

The obituary of Grace Gulkis Horan preceded her husband's folder in the file. A graduate of Wellesley College and heiress to the Gulkis fortune (Gulkis Rubber), she was mostly noted for being owner of the Star of Hunan jade. She was a victim of leukaemia.

There were perhaps forty-five clippings under Francis Xavier Flynn's name—all dating within the last eighteen months.

Fletch did not read through all the reports, but he noticed they followed a pattern.

A crime would be reported. A follow-up story would report Flynn had been assigned to it. After a few days of absolutely static news stories, in which there would be no news, there would be the "public outcry" story : Why has this crime not been solved? Impatient city editors who believed they were getting a runaround from the police were quick to report to the public its indignation. Immediately thereafter a police spokesperson would announce an imminent arrest. Not immediately thereafter, Flynn would be quoted, in response to questioning, as saying, "Nonsense. We're not arresting anybody". At first, this announcement would be followed by another "public outcry" story or one which regretfully questioned the competence of the Boston police.

Not in response, absolutely on his own time schedule, Flynn would announce an arrest. Frequently the arrest report appeared as a small item, on a back page.

Halfway through the file, references began to appear to Inspector Francis "Reluctant" Flynn. The "public outcry" and "police incompetence" stories became less frequent and then stopped altogether. The press had discovered they couldn't push Flynn. They had also discovered he was pretty good.

One of the earliest reports referred to Flynn as "formerly Chicago precinct chief of detectives".

"Do you need anything, Mister Locke?"

The young hypocrite ambled up the row between the file cabinets.

"No, thanks, Randy." Fletch shut the drawer. "I guess I'm done."

"What's the story you're working on, Mister Locke?"

"Nothing very interesting. Feature on the history of New England celebrations of the American Revolution."

"Oh."

The kid appeared to agree it wasn't very interesting. If Ralph Locke was working on such a nothing story, he wasn't very interesting, either.

"I expect you'll read it," Fletch said. "It will be under my by-line."

XVIII

F L E T C H found Jack Saunders in the city room.

Someone had handed him a wire photo, which he showed to Fletch.

It was a picture of the President of the United States trying to put on a sweater without first removing his vizored cap and sunglasses.

"That's news, uh?"

"Actually, it is," said Fletch. "I always thought he stepped into his sweaters."

Jack dropped the picture on the copy desk.

"Send it over to the Sunday feature section. Maybe they'll run it under 'Trends'."

"Jack, I'd like to see your art critic."

"So would I," said Jack. "I'm not sure I ever have. We get a lot of phone calls for him. Mostly angry. His name's Charles Wainwright."

They walked down a long, dark corridor to the back of the building.

Fletch said, "Do you remember Inspector Flynn in Chicago?"

"What Flynn? 'Reluctant' Flynn?"

"Yeah. Your copy said he was a precinct Chief of Detectives in Chicago before coming here."

"The *Star* said that?"

"Your very own newspaper."

"Frank Flynn was never in Chicago. Not two years ago. And not with that rank. I would have had to know him."

"I don't remember him, either."

"That's a mystery," said Jack.

"That's a mystery."

Charles Wainwright was the filthiest man Fletch had ever seen indoors.

His face was only relatively shaved, as if beard had been pulled out in tufts. In his fifties, particularly his nose and chin gave sustenance to many black-headed pimples. His shirt collars were turning up in decay. And on the shirt front, where the protruding stomach had stopped their fall, were evidences of at least a dozen meals. Tomato sauce had dribbled on to egg yolk.

"This is our great art critic, Charles Wainwright, Ralph," Jack said. "Charles, Ralph Locke is from Chicago, here working on a story."

Fletch braced himself to shake hands, but the slob didn't require it.

"Do what you can for him, eh?"

"Why should I?"

It took Jack a second to realize the question was serious.

"Because I ask you too."

"I don't see why I should do this man's work for him. I have work of my own to do."

Fletch said, "Actually, I'm not working on a story, Mister Wainwright. There's a rumour around Chicago that one of your Boston dealers might donate a painting to the museum there, and the publisher just asked me to stop by and have you fill me in on him."

"What do you mean? You want me to do a story on him?"

"If the guy actually donates the painting, I'd think you'd be the first person we'd call."

"Who is it?"

"Horan."

"Ronnie?"

"Is that what he's called?"

Not concealing his disgust, Jack said to Fletch, "Good luck", and left.

In the small office newspapers and books were piled everywhere, other newspapers and books thrown on top of them. And on top of that was mildew and then dust.

Wainwright sat at his desk. He rather sank among the piles.

"I've known Ronnie for years."

There was no other place in the room to sit. Although apparently permanent, none of the piles looked stable enough to bear weight.

Wainwright said, "We went to Yale together."

"Hygiene Department?"

"I guess he could give a painting to Chicago, if he wanted to. I can't think why he'd want to."

"Ah, the old city still turns a few people on. Rare beef and frequent wind, you know. Gets the blood up."

"Maybe Grace had some connection with Chicago. Maybe that's it. Her family was in the rubber business. Grace Gulkis. Gulkis Rubber."

"Not following you."

"Ronnie married Grace after the war. When he was back taking his doctorate at Harvard."

"And she's rich?"

"Was rich. She died after they had been married a few years. One of those terrible diseases. Cancer, leukaemia, something. Ronnie was heartbroken."

"And rich."

"I suppose he inherited. He started the gallery back about that time. And you don't start a gallery like that off the pay of a Harvard instructor."

"He never married again?"

"No. I've seen him with a lot of women over the years, but he never remarried. Ever hear of the Star of Hunan jade?"

"What is it?"

"It's a big rock. A famous jewel. Grace used to own it. I'm just wondering now what became of it. I must ask Ronnie."

"You'll ask him what he did with his wife's jewels?"

"There's no such thing as an improper question—just an improper answer."

"So Horan has plenty of money."

"I don't know. I don't know how much he inherited from Grace, how much went back into her family coffers. These are things you don't know about people, especially in Boston. You know what's happened to money since the 1950s."

"Heard rumours."

"He lives well, in that castle on Newbury street where he has his gallery. The top two floors are his penthouse apartment. He drives a Rolls-Royce. And anyone who drives a Rolls-Royce must be broke."

"Doesn't he have another house somewhere?"

"Maybe. I don't know."

"I mean, he can't just live over the shop."

"I've never heard he has another place."

"Was he in the service?"

"Yes. Navy. Pacific Theatre during World War Two. He was an aide to Admiral Kimberly."

"That was before he married La Gulkis?"

"Yes."

"So how did he have enough political muscle to land a cushy Admiral's aide job?"

"Well," Wainright said, "he went to Yale. A very smooth, attractive guy. Very polished."

"Where's he from, originally?"

"Some place up-country. Maine or Vermont. I forget. There's no money there. He was broke at Yale."

"I see."

"He still teaches at Harvard. Some kind of a freshman art survey course. He's written a couple of turgid books."

"Turgid?"

"Academic. I was never able to get through them. You know the kind of book where the author spends one hundred and fifty thousand words correcting the opinion of someone else who didn't matter anyway."

"Turgid."

"Your name is Ralph Locke?"

"Yeah."

"What paper?"

"*Chicago Post.*"

"You write on art?"

"Oh, no," said Fletch. "I'm a sports writer. Hockey."

"Vulgar."

"Rough."

"Primitive."

"Simple."

"Violent."

"I take it you like writing on the arts." Fletch looked around the room. "You must have a great visual sense."

The filthy man sitting in the filthy room neither confirmed nor denied the assertion.

Fletch said, "Tell me more about the Horan Gallery. Is it doing well?"

"Who knows? As an art dealer, Ronnie's the *crème de la crème.* Horan is not a walk-in gallery. He's an international art dealer making deals that are so private even the parties involved aren't sure what they're doing. He has to play very close to the chest. He could have made millions. He could be stone broke, for all I know."

"Which do you think?"

"Well, the art market in recent years has had extraordinary ups and downs. First, the Japanese came along and invested heavily. Then, some of them had to dump on the market. Then Arabs came along, trying to bury petrodollars. Many Japanese weren't deeply schooled in Western art. And Islam has a distinct prejudice against representations of the human or animate figure. So there have been funny, unpredictable distortions in the market. Plus, of course, the art market reflects every distortion in the nature of money itself. Some people have made killings off the market. Others have gotten badly stuck."

"And you don't know which has been Horan's experience."

"No. But I'm interested to hear he might give a painting to Chicago. I might use the item in my column."

"By all means, do," said Fletch. "I'm very grateful to you for all your help."

XIX

F L E T C H led the plainclothesmen through Friday evening commuter traffic back to his apartment house.

After sharing Charles Wainwright's critical vision, Fletch felt badly in need of a wash.

Taking his complimentary copy of the *Boston Star* with him (a quarter of the front page was devoted to the bathtub murder of the City Councilperson), Fletch walked up the five flights of stairs which squared the lobby elevator shaft and quietly let himself in the front door of his apartment.

Mignon did not bark.

After he washed, he went through the front door again, closing it quietly behind him.

He pushed the button for the elevator. It creaked up to the sixth floor.

He pulled open the iron-grilled doors. They clanged shut on their own weights.

After he waited a moment, he rang the bell to apartment 6A.

It took another moment for Joan Winslow to collect herself and open the door.

"I'm afraid I've locked myself out," Fletch said. "By any chance do you have a key to 6B?"

The smell of gin was not stale, but it was mixed with the odour of an air purifier.

From beside the skirt of Joan's housecoat, Mignon was looking at him with her usual polite courtesy.

"Who are you?" Joan asked.

"Peter Fletcher. I'm using Bart's apartment. We met in the elevator yesterday."

"Oh, yes." She lurched heavily on her left foot as she turned to the small hall table. "You're the man Bart dumped the body on."

"Ma'am?"

The drawer of the hall table held many keys.

"The police were here. An enormous man. Name of Wynn, or something."

"Flynn."

"He spoke so softly I could hardly hear him. Came this morning. He showed me a picture of the murdered girl. I forget her name."

"Ruth Fryer."

"Yes."

She stirred her hand through the key drawer.

Fletch said, "Yes?"

She pulled out a key with a white tag attached. It read, "Bart's—6B."

"There it is."

She lurched towards the doorway, apparently thinking Fletch was still standing in it.

"Oh," she said, finding him. "Now use this key and give it right back to me so next time one of you lock yourselves out I'll have it."

Key in hand, Fletch asked, "Did you let anyone into the apartment Tuesday night?"

"No. Of course not. I've never let anyone into that apartment. Except Bart. Lucy. And now you. Anyway, I wasn't here Tuesday night. I had drinks and dinner with some friends."

"Where did you have drinks?"

"Bullfinch Pub." She knew she was repeating herself. "Just up the street."

"I see."

"That's where I saw Bart. And the girl."

Fletch crossed the small hall and opened the door to 6B with Joan Winslow's key.

Handing it back to her, he asked, "Was the girl you saw with Bart Tuesday night the same girl in the photograph the police showed you?"

"Yes," Joan Winslow said. "Of course."

"Did you tell the police that?"

"Certainly. I'd tell anybody that."

She whisked Mignon behind her with the long skirt of her houserobe.

"Come in," she said. "It's drinks time."

"Thank you."

"Don't you want a drink?"

"I'll be right with you."

Fletch crossed the small elevator landing, closed the door to his apartment, and returned to Joan's. He closed the door behind him.

Swaying over a well-stocked bar in the living room, her face was that of a child at a soda counter.

Her living room was a counterpart of Connors', in its large size and basic solidity, but far more feminine. Instead of polished leathers and dark woods the upholstery was white and blue and pink, the furniture light and spindly. The paintings on the walls were originals, imitative modern junk.

"Seeing it's Friday night, shall we have a martini? Why don't you make it?" She waved her hand airily at the bar. "Men make martinis so much better than women do."

"Oh, yes?"

She placed the ice bucket centrally on the service table.

"I'll make crackers and cheese," she said.

She walked flat-footed, placing most of her weight on the heels of her house slippers, prepared at each step to prevent a fall sideways. Joan Winslow was accustomed to being crocked.

"Well." On the divan, her legs curled up under her houserobe, she bit into a bare cracker. "Isn't this nice?"

Fletch poured.

"Have you known the Connorses long?"

"Years. Ever since they were married. The apartment next door was being prepared for them while they were on their honeymoon and I was in Nevada getting a divorce. We all arrived back within a day or two of each other and just fell into each other's arms."

"You hadn't known each other before?"

"No, indeed. If I had laid eyes on Bart Connors before Lucy, she wouldn't have had a chance. He was a darling. And we'd all be much better off."

She took the tiniest sip of her martini.

"Um, good. Men can make better martinis than women."

"I used a little vermouth."

"You see—what's your name, Peter? That doesn't seem right to me, somehow, but I'll use it—they were just getting used to marriage, and I was just getting used to divorce. My husband, a structural engineer, had accepted a contract in Latin America, in Costa Rica, the year before. The poor, empty-headed boob remarried there. I found out some months later. I mean, I had no choice but to divorce him, did I? Why put a person in jail just because he's a booby? Don't you think it was the best thing to do?"

"Absolutely," Fletch said firmly.

"Only the Connorses never did get used to marriage." She drank half her martini in a single swallow. "And I have never gotten used to divorce."

The woman, at the most, was in her early forties. She had probably been attractive, in a petite, helpless, feminine way. She probably could be again, if she would put down her glass.

"At first," she continued, "it was great fun. They didn't know the building, or the district. I got the janitorial service to work for them—there was always something abrasive about Lucy—and found them a string of apartment cleaners. People were doing things for the Connorses because I asked them to. Lucy quite turned people off."

She finished her drink. Fletch did not pour her another.

"After a year or so, it was pretty obvious she turned Bart off, too. When I had a dinner party, I usually had the Connorses as guests. They invited me, with or without escort, when they were throwing a bash. What could we do, really? There are only two apartments on this floor, and we were friends. We had to be."

She poured herself a fresh drink.

"One night, after they had been here for dinner, Bart came back. All the other guests had gone. We had a nightcap. A big one. We both had too much to drink. Lucy was frigid, he said. Always had been. Or so he thought.

"There was a year of psychiatry for her. During that time, I sort of played psychiatrist for Bart. He'd come over late at night. We'd have a drink, and talk. As you can imagine, Lucy became a little cool with me. I could never make out whether it was because I was intimate with the family secrets, or because I was getting too much attention from Bart. I can tell you one thing. During all that time, and it went on for a long time, Bart was completely faithful to Lucy. He couldn't have been otherwise, without his telling me. I was his good friend. His drinking buddy.

"Lucy dropped psychiatry after a while. Bart found her another shrink, but she refused to go. You see, I think she had discovered what the so-called problem was.

"Then I noticed a young woman coming in and out of the apartment house, and it sort of puzzled me, as I knew no one had moved in. I saw her during the daytime. Then I realized she was going to 6B. I assumed it was some old friend of Lucy's. Then I met her at a cocktail party at the Connorses. Her name is Marsha Hauptmann. It was announced she and Lucy were starting a boutique together. How nice. All very reasonable.

"Until the servant we had in common in those days—that was before Mrs. Sawyer, who now comes to me on Tuesdays and Fridays, she just left, and you on Wednesdays and Saturdays—told me Lucy and Marsha were taking showers together! How else can I say it? They were using the bed together.

"Incidentally, I fired the person who told me that. Servants must not be allowed to gossip in the neighbourhood. And, in truth, I had not wanted to know any such thing. Do you believe that?"

"Of course," Fletch said.

"Then I did rather a stupid thing. I thought it was right at the time. I never told Bart. We had always been strictly honest with each other, but I just couldn't tell him that. I thought the news coming from me would destroy his faith in his own manliness, his own perceptions, if you see what I mean. He had to find out by himself. Instead, I encouraged infidelity."

"With you?"

"I was in love with Bart. Please, would you pour me another touch more?"

Fletch poured into her glass.

"I'm ashamed to say I did," she said. "I had never been a seductress before, although I had been seduced enough. I'm afraid I was rather clumsy at it. Bart couldn't understand. He thought of me as a friend of Lucy's. I was his old drinking buddy. Suddenly, I turn all hot and passionate. I should say, I let him see how hot and passionate I always had been towards him.

"He rejected me. There's no other way to say that, either.

"Months went by. No more mutual dinner parties. No more drinking with Bart.

"I guess finally she told him she was leaving him for another woman. The poor jerk still hadn't caught on."

Fletch said, "After Lucy accepted her lesbianism, why did she wait so long before divorcing Bart?"

"Those adjustments take time, I expect. Maybe she thought it was a momentary thing. She had been told she was frigid enough times, by Bart and Bart's psychiatrists. I knew that. Here was a person who turned her on. It happened to be another girl.

"Anyway," Joan continued, "Lucy had nothing and Bart is rich. His father built Wardor-Rand, you know. Bart inherited most of it. Haven't you noticed the paintings in his apartment? You can't buy those with cheesecake. His father ended his days being our ambassador to Australia."

"I see," Fletch said. "But ultimately, she did tell him, and she told him the truth."

"I guess so. Can you realize what that must do to a man? Realize he's been married to a girl who doesn't, who can't have the slightest interest in him, sexually?"

"She could have."

"I'm sure it didn't seem that way to Bart. Every man wants to believe he's married to a red-hot mama, who loves him sexually. My husband did. Twice, apparently. To discover your wife prefers girls—to the point where she is leaving you for a girl— can't do much for your ego, no matter how modern you are."

"I guess not."

"And I'm sure Bart tried to be understanding. He would."

"Were the facts of this affair public?"

"Everyone knew about it. Everyone in our circle. That's how I knew the great moment of revelation had come. By that time, you see, neither one of them was talking to me."

"He must have felt a little foolish."

"Innocent, anyway. Bart, despite his age, was a very innocent man. He went to one of the up-country colleges. Was never in the service. Worked like hell through law school and during his first years at the firm, having to work with Wardor-Rand simultaneously. His father was dead. When he married Lucy, he was very naive."

"He isn't now."

She offered the plate of bare crackers to Fletch. There was no cheese anywhere in sight.

He refused them.

"So why do you still hate Bart?" he asked.

"Hate him? Did I say I hate him? I suppose I do.

"After the incident, the revelation, he didn't come to me. I waited, politely.

"Then one day I heard him on the landing. I opened my door and put my arms out to him. I guess I was crying. It was morning. I said, 'Oh, Bart, I'm so sorry'. I tried to hug him. He took my arms away from around his neck."

"He rejected you again."

"He even said something rather cutting about my drinking habits. After all the drinks I had poured nursing him. Something unforgiveable."

Fletch said, "I expect the poor guy was feeling a little sour on all womanhood at that moment."

"It's not that." Her tears were as big as drops of gin. "He not only rejected me as a woman. That I could understand, at the moment. What hurts is that he rejected me as a friend."

"I see."

Unabashed, Joan continued talking through her tears, her whole mouth working to get the words out comprehensibly.

"Then there was that endless stream of girls who poured through here. Pony tails. Frizzy hair. Blue jeans. Little skirts. It's been going on for months."

Fletch waited for her breathing to become more regular.

"So you think he finally killed one of them."

"Of course, he did. The bastard."

She flat-heeled over to the serving table and poured herself a slug of straight gin and poured it down her throat.

"It wasn't any girl he was killing. Any Ruthie what's-her-name. It was Lucy. He was killing Lucy."

For a moment, Fletch sat, saying nothing.

Mignon, sitting on the divan, was looking anxiously at her mistress.

Finally, Fletch said, "Is there anything I can do for you?"

"No." She brushed hair back from her forehead. "I think I'll take a bath and go to bed."

"No supper?"

"I'm too tired."

Fletch dropped her key to Bart's apartment on the coffee table.

"We can get a sandwich somewhere. It's early yet. What about this pub you've mentioned? Up the street."

"Really," she said. "I'm much too tired. The police were here this morning. About Bart."

"I understand." Standing up, he said, "Someday I'd like to take Mignon for a nice long walk."

"She'd love that."

Joan Winslow showed him to the door. Her face looked dreadful.

"Good night."

When he got to his own door he realized that supposedly he didn't have the key.

Her door closed.

He shrugged, took his own key out of his pocket, and let himself in.

X X

FLETCH was still wondering about the source of his own supper, trying to remember the name of the pub up the street, when his doorbell rang.

"Oh, my God."

The Countess de Grassi was standing among her luggage on the landing.

A head with a taxi driver's hat on it was descending down the elevator shaft.

"Eighteen, twenty miles you say! It's no eighteen, twenty miles."

"I said it wasn't."

"All the time you lie, Flesh." She tried, but not very hard, to pick up one of her suitcases, the biggest. "A nice man let me in downstairs."

"Sylvia, what do you think you're doing?"

Sylvia could turn an elevator landing into a stage.

"You say Ritz too expensive for me." Helplessness was expressed by widened eyes, arms thrown wide—even her cleavage seemed wider. "You right. They present me bill."

"Did you pay it?"

"Of course I pay it. You think the Countess de Grassi some sort of crook? Everybody rob the Countess de Grassi. The Countess de Grassi rob no one!"

Fletch remained in the centre of the doorway.

"But why did you come here?"

"Why do I come here? What you think? Why should Countess de Grassi stay in too-expensive hotel when her son-in-law live around corner in magnificent apartment?"

"I'm not your son-in-law. Ye gods."

"You marry Andy, you become my son-in-law. You become member de Grassi family. I, Countess de Grassi!"

"I've heard." He faltered back a step. "What the hell is this? Son-in-step-law? Step-son-in-law? Son-in-law-step?"

"No! No English double-talk in American, please."

"Me? Wouldn't think of it."

She entered through the small space his body left in the doorway.

He closed the door on her luggage.

"Very nice." Her quick glance through the living room door was followed by a quick glance through the den door. "Okay enough. Very nice."

"Sylvia, there are other hotels."

"Not for the Countess de Grassi. Always number one place. What would poor, dead Menti say if Countess de Grassi stay in fleabag?"

"I think he'd probably say, 'Thank God. I left a lousy estate.' "

"He left no lousy estate. He left magnificent estate. My paintings!"

"There are more middle-class hotels, Sylvia."

"Middle-class? You crazy in the head, you bull-shitting son of a bitch. The Countess de Grassi is not middle-class."

"I see."

She flounced the white gloves in her hands, substituting the action for removing them. They had never been on. It was doubtful they would fit over her rather impressive diamond ring.

"Now. Where my room?"

"Sylvia, you wouldn't be here just to keep an eye on me, would you?"

"Eye on you? Devil eye on you!"

Her eyes spat into his.

"Because, honestly, I'm not doing anything about your paintings. I know nothing about your paintings." Fletch thought a shout would be worth trying. "I'm here researching a book about an American artist, and you'd be in my way!"

"You bet your cock I'll be in your way!" One should never try to outshout a Brazilian who had been married to both a Frenchman and an Italian. And who was not middle-class. "You no make one move without me! I at the hotel! I might as well be in Rome! In Livorno! I'm not here to buy you a drink and go away again! I'm here to catch my paintings!"

"Sylvia, I know nothing about your paintings."

"Now. Where is my room? Servants can bring in the luggage."

"Sylvia, there are no servants."

"No servants! Always you lie. Who answered your phone the other day? The woman who puts her eyelashes in the refrigerator!"

"Oh, boy."

The Countess de Grassi marched down the corridor to the bedrooms, snapping on lights as she went.

While Fletch was still in the reception hall, the telephone rang. He answered it in the den.

"Hello, Mister Fletcher?"

"Yeah."

"This is Mister Horan, of the Horan Gallery."

"Oh, yes."

"Sorry to bother you on a Friday night, especially after seven, but I thought you'd be pleased to hear my good news."

"Oh?"

"Yes. I've succeeded in locating the painting you were interested in, Picasso's 'Vino, Viola, Mademoiselle'."

"That's wonderful."

"I've talked with the present owner. Like the rest of us, I guess, he's suffering somewhat from a shortage of cash, and I think he was rather pleased that someone has come forward at this time with an interest in buying it. I suggested to him that as you had sought the painting out, he might get a slightly higher price than if he were simply to offer it on the market himself now or in the near future."

"I hope you didn't make his mouth water too much."

"No, no. Simply a negotiating device. But of course a seller does do better when a negotiation is initiated by the buyer. You do understand."

"Of course."

"He does slightly better. If, after we see the painting, you are still interested in its purchase, I will do my best to get it for you at the most reasonable price."

"Tell me, Mister Horan, where is the painting?" There was a hesitation on the phone. "Who is its present owner?"

"Well, I don't usually like to answer that question. I'm a private dealer."

Fletch said nothing.

Horan said, "I guess there's no reason why I shouldn't answer you, in this instance. The painting is owned by a man named Cooney. In Dallas, Texas."

"Texas. Texas is still big in the art market, eh?"

"There are some superb private collections in Texas. Mister Cooney has not been an active collector, to my knowledge, but he does have this piece and some others I know of. The Barclough Bank in Nassau has given you a credit reference more than adequate. Therefore, I have asked Mister Cooney to fly the painting up for our inspection. It should be here by morning."

"The painting is coming here?"

"It should already be on its way. I tried to get you by phone this afternoon. Truth is, I had to spend considerable time advising Mister Cooney on the work's proper crating and insurance."

"I'm very surprised the picture is coming here."

"Well, I want to see it myself. If it's authentic I might want to purchase it myself, or find another purchaser for it, should you decide not to purchase it. Once an owner gets over what might be called a psychological hump and makes the basic decision that he might consider selling an object of art, if the price is right—as our Mister Cooney did this afternoon after lunch in Dallas—then a dealer should go forward with him and arrange a sale."

"You did all this by telephone?"

"Oh, yes. I'm not unknown in Texas."

"Well, that's wonderful. What else can you tell me about Mister Cooney?"

"Not much. I was put on to him by a curator, friend of mine, at the Dallas Museum. My source knew Cooney owned a Picasso of your general description, but had never seen it. I called Mister Cooney last night and asked him bluntly if he owned a Picasso entitled 'Vino, Viola, Mademoiselle', an impossible title. I gather he dropped his bourbon bottle. He answered in the affirmative. I said I might have a purchaser for it. He thought about it overnight. I believe he's in ranching. Has something like eight children."

"That's why he needs some cash, right?"

"In any case, Mister Fletcher, albeit tomorrow is Saturday, I believe if you came here—is nine-thirty too early?—we could look at the painting together and perhaps make Mister Cooney an offer before the bourbon begins to flow again."

"Yes. That would be fine. You say the painting is coming by air tonight?"

"Yes. If all goes well. If it's not here in the morning, I'll give you a ring. But I'm sure it will be here."

Fletch said, "Okay, I'll see you in the morning."

Sylvia stood in the doorway to the den.

"You'll see who in the morning?"

At least she had not been listening on the extension.

"I have to see a man about a horse."

"A Degas horse?"

"No, Sylvia. A pinto."

"What is this, pinto horse. A painted horse, right?"

Now in a more kittenish manner, she sat in one of the leather chairs.

"What about my dinner?" she said.

"What about it?"

"No servants. Don't you expect me to eat, Flesh? I am your guest!"

"Right," Fletch said. "You've never tasted my cooking, have you?"

"You cook?"

"Like a dream." He kissed the tips of his fingers and exploded them before his face. "Um! Better than the Ritz! Let's see." Thoughtfully, he paced the small room. "To begin with, a *potage au cresson*, yes? *Timbales de foies de volaille.* Good! *Homard à l'americaine!* Then, of course, *a fricassée de poulet à l'indienne*, with *pois frais en braisage.* What could be better! Eh? For dessert, *charlotte Chantilly, aux framboises!* Splendid!" He considered her anxiously. "Would that be all right, do you think? Countess?"

"It sounds all right."

"Of course, it will take me some time."

"I'm used to eating late. I want to see these things you cook."

"I'd offer you a drink, but of course, I never would before such a dinner."

"Of course not. I'll take nothing to drink."

"You sit right there. I'll get busy in the kitchen."

Briskly, Fletch crossed the reception hall and went through the swing door to the kitchen.

He also went through the kitchen, out of its back door, and down the stairs to the alley.

He ran to the garage on River Street.

Not taking time to figure a new route to 60 Newbury Street, he drove down Beacon Street, past his own apartment. The two plainclothesmen in the parked car across from 152 Beacon Street looked like bags of laundry. But they had their eyes firmly on the front door of the apartment house. Fletch scratched his left temple while passing them.

He turned left on Arlington Street and right on Newbury. Double parking outside a pharmacy, he ran in and ordered two sandwiches and some soft drinks to go. He also ordered two cups of coffee.

There was a place to park diagonally across the street from the Horan Gallery.

He turned off his lights and engine and settled down to wait.

It was then he realized he would need more than his suit jacket. He was cold.

Within twenty minutes the garage doors at 60 Newbury Street opened. Fletch saw the grille of a Rolls-Royce with its headlights on.

The sixty-year-old houseman, or gallery assistant or whatever he was, closed the doors after the Rolls pulled out.

There was only one way the Rolls could go on Newbury Street, it being a one-way west, and the car went west.

In the van Fletch followed Horan in the Rolls.

They went by several cross-streets. They went west to the end of Newbury Street.

After stopping at a red light, they crossed Massachusetts Avenue and dipped down a ramp on to the Massachusetts Turnpike Extension. And kept going west.

The Rolls proceeded at a stately fifty-five miles per hour. It went through a toll booth, making its proper genuflection to the exact change machine, and continued westward.

It curved right before the second toll booth. "WESTON", Fletch read, "128 NORTH/SOUTH".

At the end of the off-ramp, there was another toll booth.

In his own lane, Fletch caught up to Horan. He waited a moment before throwing change out of the window, as if he were having trouble finding the exact change.

The Rolls preceded him on to the Weston Road.

After stopping at a light, the two vehicles veered right. The road from there curved and climbed gently, past woods, a golf course, well-spaced antique farmhouses, and more contemporary estate houses.

Fletch dared not let the Rolls' tail-lights get more than one hundred and fifty metres ahead of him.

Even that was almost too much, on that road.

After a curve the tail-lights were no longer ahead of him. Slowing imperceptibly, Fletch saw a car going through woods down a driveway to his left. The headlights were high and round, the shape of the car boxy, the tail-lights huge. It had to be the Rolls.

Fletch drove around the next curve and pulled over. He left his parking lights on.

He ran along the soft shoulder of the road back to the driveway he thought Horan had taken. The mailbox read MILLER.

Lights in a house further down to his left went on.

The mailbox on that driveway read HORAN.

Stepping around in the dark, he explored the area across from the driveway.

There was a break in the stone wall, with a rusty chain across it. The wall was only two metres from the road.

Fletch returned to his truck and turned it around.

Before reversing, to put the back bumper of his truck against the chain, he turned out its headlights.

The chain snapped easily.

Crunching through brush, Fletch backed up, turned the wheel, and then drove forward to the wall.

Through a light screen of brush in front of him, he had a perfect view of the Horan driveway.

In the silent dark, he had one sandwich and a cup of coffee.

He watched the lights go out in the Horan house. At a quarter to twelve all the lights were out in the neighbours' house.

At one-thirty, Fletch walked up the shoulder of Horan's gravel driveway. Moonlight came and went through the clouds.

After a patch of woods, a lawn appeared to the left, in front of the house. It had two levels. The upper level apparently was used as a patio. Under a green striped awning, white, wrought-iron furniture remained outdoors in October.

The house was a rather imposing, three-storied structure. Its slate roof reflected moonlight.

Going around the right of the house, Fletch had to cross a patch of gravel. He took off his shoes to do so.

A garage was connected to the house.

Around the garage ran a dirt car track, to an unused, three-sided tractor shed. The extensive gardens at the back of the house had fallen into decay.

He examined the windows at the back of the house. All, including the windows in the kitchen door, were wired with a burglar alarm system.

Woods came up to the far side of the house.

Fletch returned to his van and had his second sandwich and the cold coffee.

By three-thirty he was cold enough to look in the back of the van for something to wrap around himself, although he was sure there was nothing there.

In fact, the painters had left a long piece of tarpaulin. The splattered paint on it was dry to the touch.

Returning to the driver's seat, he wrapped the tarpaulin around him.

He was getting comfortably warm when dawn arrived.

Almost immediately, rain sounded against the truck's roof. It obscured vision through the windshield.

Turning on the ignition, but not the engine. Fletch sent the wipers over the windshield every few minutes.

At a quarter past eight, he saw the grille of the Rolls-Royce in the driveway opposite.

It had been Fletch's plan to pull the truck further back into the woods if he had forewarning of Horan's departure. He had had none.

He hoped the combination of the rain and the screen of brush in front of him protected him somewhat from being seen.

The Rolls did not stop. It turned right, without hesitation, back the way it had come the night before.

After Horan went around the curve, Fletch extricated the truck from the bushes and followed him.

He followed him back to 60 Newbury Street.

Fletch was parked—halfway down the block—before the manservant opened the garage in response to Horan's horn. The Rolls backed across the sidewalk into the garage.

It was ten minutes to nine, Saturday morning.

At nine-fifteen, Fletch drove to the pharmacy. There he bought a razor, a blade, and a can of shaving foam. He also bought a cup of tea to go.

In the truck he loosened his collar, threw out the tea bag, and, using the tarpaulin, as well as the razor, the blade, the shaving foam, and the tea, shaved himself.

At nine-thirty he rang the doorbell of the Horan Gallery.

XXI

T H E Picasso was on the easel in Horan's office.

"Ah, good morning, Mister Fletcher. Wet morning."

"'Fraid I came away without my raincoat." The weather would take the blame for his dishevelled appearance. "Hard to get a taxi in the rain."

"Always," sympathized the impeccable Ronald Horan. "Well. There it is."

Fletch had stopped in front of the painting.

Damned fool title but what could the painting be called but "Vino, Viola, Mademoiselle"? The basic shape was repeated three times. The first image, or the fourth, was the true shape.

"Magnificent," he said.

"I believe I can guarantee its authenticity."

"I'm speechless," Fletch said.

"I'm curious as to why you want to purchase this piece in particular? I'm always curious about that."

"I saw a slide of it," Fletch said, "at a little showing in Cannes, sometime well after Picasso's death. It just sped by with a lot of other slides. It struck me as possibly the key Cubist work, even more refined than others of the same theme."

Horan was looking at the painting as well.

"You may be right," he said.

"But let's not tell Mister Cooney."

Fletch walked around the easel. "It's all right? It arrived without damage?"

"No damage at all." Horan joined him behind the painting. "And, I may add, I believe this is the original stretcher. Although it may not be."

"You picked it up at the airport yourself?"

Horan moved to the front of the painting.

"I rather indicated to Mister Cooney we'd be in touch with him sometime early today. Although we needn't be, of course. It's up to you."

"What's your advice?"

"You might start with six hundred and fifty thousand dollars."

Fletch wandered to a chair from which he could see both Horan and the painting.

"You say Mister Cooney is not an active collector?"

"Well, he's not in the business of collecting," Horan answered. "I've bought one or two other things from him in the last year or two. They've always proven to be right."

"You've bought two other paintings from him within the last two years?"

"As I say, the man doesn't have a professional reputation to uphold, as a dealer would have, or a museum, but his other sales, at least through this gallery, have been entirely successful."

Tall, slim, suave, greying Horan prowled the rug, arms behind his back, in an attitude of respectful waiting.

Quietly, firmly, Fletch said, "I'm interested in the painting's provenance."

"Ah!" Horan responded as if a whole new topic had been introduced—an original question from a slow student. "I'm not sure you'll be entirely satisfied there."

"No?"

"You see, in many private sales provenance is not offered." The man was lecturing again. "Especially in a case of this sort. There is no record of this painting in existence—at least none I've been able to find. Of far more importance, there appears to be no record of this painting's ever having left another country, or ever having entered this country. Governments, with their taxes and other requirements, their increasing interest in preserving national cultural objects, these days, you know, can be a bit sticky."

"I know. Which, of course, makes my having the provenance of this painting all the more important."

"Yes, I can see that. You live in Italy, don't you?"

"I sometimes do."

"Of course, we can ask Mister Cooney the provenance."

"You haven't done so?"

"I know what he'll say."

"Let me guess," said Fletch. "He'll say he bought it from a reputable dealer in Switzerland sometime in the past, and he doesn't remember precisely when."

"Well, yes." Horan was pleased by the slow student's perceptive answer. "I expect that's what he would say."

"There are more reputable art dealers in Switzerland than there are citizens of France. Piled on top of each other, they are that nation's national culture."

"As I guess you know, Swiss dealers seldom confirm sales."

"I think we should ask, Mister Horan."

"By all means, we should."

"I wish to know the source, and the history of this painting."

"Of course, when a provenance isn't offered, Mister Fletcher...."

"I would be derelict in not asking for the provenance."

"You said you represent yourself?"

"I would be derelict in my obligations to myself, my estate, as well as to those parts of the art world which consider their responsibilities. Frankly, I'm fairly shocked you cannot say you have already asked for a complete provenance."

Below Horan's silver-streaked temples appeared a flush of red.

"I don't think you understand, Mister Fletcher, how usual this situation is. Very common, indeed. Art is the international language. It is also an international currency. The art market, by its nature, is international. It cannot recognize arbitrary, national borders. Governments have been poking more and more into matters which are beyond their natural province. People must insist upon privacy in their affairs, especially in aesthetic matters."

"Ah, yes."

"You remember, I'm sure, the deluge of art objects flooding

out of Britain in late 1975, as a result of incredible legislative mistakes by the Labour government. Were you unsympathetic?"

"I understood the movement."

"Incidentally, it is entirely possible 'Vino, Viola, Mademoiselle' is one of those objects of art which found its way here from Britain."

"It's also possible it's not. In any case, even if it is, I must protect myself, Mister Horan."

"My dear Mister Fletcher! You are protected. Entirely protected. We are not new in this business. After spending a little more time with this painting, I'm sure I will have no hesitation in authenticating it. If you wish a second authentication, or even a third, such can be arranged locally within a matter of days, if not hours."

"Very good of you."

"You will have bought the painting through the Horan Gallery in Boston, with proper authentication. My reputation has never been questioned. If asked, which I doubt I would be, I will state happily the seller is James Cooney, of Dallas, Texas. When asked, he, in turn. . . ."

". . . will say he bought it sometime in the past from a reputable dealer in Switzerland," Fletch said. "And the reputable dealer in Switzerland will refuse to come forward with the record, which is his right, as a Swiss citizen."

"Bless the Swiss," said Horan. "They still have some sense of privacy left—although it is dissipating."

"I understand all this, Mister Horan."

"In the meantime, and forever, your investment is absolutely protected."

"It remains my obligation to ask the question. I want to know where Cooney got the painting, even if it is in the nature of private, undocumented information."

"Yes. Of course, you're right, Mister Fletcher. We should ask the question. In the meantime, would you care to mention a specific price to Mister Cooney?"

Horan stepped behind his Louis Seize desk to answer the telephone. The ring had been muffled.

"Hello? Yes, this is Mister Horan. . . . Who wishes to speak to me? . . . Hello? No, operator, no . . . I will accept no calls from anyone in Chicago today. . . . This is the third call I've had from the *Chicago Tribune* . . . I have already denied that story. . . . What's your name? . . . Mister Potok? . . . Two others of your reporters have already called here this morning, Mister Potok. How many times do I have to deny a story? ... I am not giving, nor have I ever intended to give a painting to the Chicago museum.... What do you mean, what painting am I *not* going to give? My God.... I have no idea where the Boston newspaper got the story. I believe it was the *Star*. I haven't read the story. I expect it was their idiot critic, Charles Wainwright, who has never gotten anything right.... Listen, Mister Potok, I am not giving a painting to the Chicago museum; I never intended to give a painting to the Chicago museum.... I never will give a painting to the Chicago museum.... What do you mean? I have nothing against the Chicago museum.... Mister Potok, I am running out of patience. The story is entirely fallacious. Please don't call here again."

His footfalls on the rug repeated the quiet firmness with which he had hung up the phone.

"Some damn fool Boston newspaper reported I am going to give a painting to the Chicago museum." Horan shook his head. "Totally untrue. Where do they get things like that?"

"There's no accounting for the press," said Fletch.

"We were discussing price."

Fletch stood. He remembered he didn't have a coat.

"Yes. We were," said Fletch." I think we might offer Mister Cooney two hundred and seventy-five thousand dollars."

Horan looked slapped.

"That would be totally unacceptable."

"I know. I'll go higher, of course. But tell Mister Cooney I am deeply anxious about the source of this painting."

"I doubt he'll talk in response to such an offer."

"He might talk—a lot."

XXII

"WHO's there?"

"The big, bad pomegranate."

It was eleven-thirty Saturday morning.

Fletch had had to go a little out of his way to find a hardware store on his way home from Newbury Street. He had bought a screwdriver, a pair of pliers, and a small can of household oil —all of which he had left in the truck.

After putting the truck in the River Street garage, he had cut through the alley and up the iron, cement-walled back stairs to his apartment.

He had forgotten Mrs. Sawyer would be there. Naturally, she had locked the back door.

"You go away," she shouted through the door. "Nothing gets picked up on Saturdays."

"It's Mister Fletcher, Mrs. Sawyer! Please open up."

"What are you doing out there?"

The two bolts slid free of the door.

"Well, look at you!" she said. "Out caterwauling all night! Where's your coat? You're wet like a puppy."

"Good morning."

"You have a European countess sleeping in your own bed, and you're not even home to enjoy it."

"In my bed?"

"She calls herself the Countess del Gassey."

"She should."

"I've never seen so much luggage. She expect to be buried here?"

"She slept in my bed?"

"Didn't you leave her there?"

"I did not. Where is she?"

"She said something about going shopping. Then she said something about going to the museum and visiting some galleries."

"Great."

"I fed her, and she's gone. Mercy, Lord, was she hungry! You'd think no one had fed her in a month."

"No one has." The bright, white kitchen was a complete contrast to the cold, dark, wet truck. "I'm wet."

"Your hair looks like you spent the night tunnelling through a haystack. Maybe that's what you were doing. You want something to eat?"

"Sure would. Where are the countess's things?"

"You'll see. All over the apartment. I never met such a bossy woman. She talked to me like I was a platoon."

"Would you move everything of hers into a guest room, please? And then close the door. Tight."

"I'm not sure it will all fit! You want breakfast, or lunch?"

"Anything warm would be great. By the way, where are the telephone books?"

After standing in a warm shower, he sat on the edge of his bed and checked all the local telephone books.

There was no listing for Lucy Connors.

However, there was a listing, on Fenton Street, in Brookline, for Marsha Hauptmann.

He dialled the number and waited through four rings.

"Hello?"

"Hello. This is Martin Head, of *Très Magazine*. Is Ms. Connors there?"

Fletch guessed it was Ms. Hauptmann who said, "Just a moment, please."

Another voice came on the line. "Hello?"

"Ms. Connors, this is Martin Head, of *Très Magazine*. I've been trying your number all week."

"Yes?"

"Ms. Connors, I'd appreciate your listening very carefully to what I have to say, and see if you can't agree to it."

"I doubt I will."

"Please. You'll see our intention is good and, with your co-operation, the result may be good."

"You've got me mystified. I don't read your magazine."

"We would like to do a sensitive, personal story—without mentioning any names, or using any photographs—on women who have declared themselves lesbian, especially after having gone through a few years of married life."

"Where did you get my name?"

"Your husband."

"Bart's in Italy. I can't believe that."

"We met him Tuesday night in Montreal. Apparently he's far more understanding, or trying to be far more understanding, than many husbands in similar circumstances we have met."

"Bart? I suppose so."

"I believe you could give our readers some genuinely sensitive insights into what you've been through—some real understanding. You'd be an ideal interview."

"I don't think so. Is it Mister Head?"

"Martin."

"Does this have anything to do with the murder?"

"What murder?"

"There was a murder in my husband's apartment the other night. I wouldn't want to comment on it. It's perfectly irrelevant."

"I didn't know about that." Fletch's eyes wandered around Lucy and Bart Connors' old bedroom. "If it's irrelevant, why should it be mentioned?"

"I don't think so, Martin. This has been bad enough, without publicity."

"Lucy, think how bad it is for other women in the circumstances you were in. I daresay you felt pretty alone, going through it."

"Certainly did."

"It sometimes helps to be able to read that someone else has been through it. You've resolved your problems, fairly successfully, I gather. . . ."

"You're a very convincing fella, Martin."

"Furthermore, I guarantee you, there will be no personal publicity. You'll be referred to as 'Ms. C', period. Nice, tasteful drawings, probably abstracts, will be made up as illustrations."

"And what if you don't?"

"You can sue us. We know we're trespassing here on personal, intimate affairs. We're doing a story on your feelings, rather than the facts. We're not out to expose anybody, or anything."

"I see. Would you let me read the story and okay it before it's published?"

"We don't like to do that. The editors sort of feel that's their job."

"I won't talk to you unless I see the story before it's published."

Fletch forced himself to hesitate. "Okay, Lucy. I agree. It will have to be between us, but I'll let you see the story before I hand it in. When can I see you?"

"Marsha and I are going shopping this afternoon if this rain ever lets up. And we're seeing friends tonight."

"May I come tomorrow morning?"

"Okay. About ten?"

"Ten-thirty. 58 Fenton Street?"

"Apartment 42."

"Will Ms. Hauptmann be there?"

"You bet. You goof up one little bit, Babe, and we'll both stomp you."

XXIII

A F T E R steak and eggs, provided and prepared by Mrs. Sawyer, Fletch got into his freshly made bed with yesterday's edition of the *Boston Star.*

The murder of Ruth Fryer received little space compared to the space devoted to the City Councilperson's murder. Obviously there was no new news concerning Ruth Fryer's murder. The City Councilperson's murder was reported in the greatest detail, together with her full biography, with pictures of her throughout her career, a personal recollection piece by the paper's chief local reporter, a sidebar of quotes from notables, political and nonpolitical, friends and enemies, all conspicuously generous. She was a jowly, mean-eyed woman. Indeed, she must have been an unpleasant sight, bloody in her bath.

After more than an hour, Fletch saw an advertisement for an Alec Guinness matinée double bill, *The Lavender Hill Mob* and *The Man in the White Suit.* It was the right thing to do, on a rainy Saturday afternoon. According to his map, the theatre was not far.

While he was dressing in slacks, loafers, open shirt, sweater and tweed jacket, he heard the door buzzers ring and presumed it was some enterprise of Mrs. Sawyer. She was trying to restock the kitchen shelves.

Coming down the corridor, then, he was surprised to see Inspector Flynn in the hall. His Irish-knit sweater made his chest and shoulders look even more huge, his head even more minute.

"Ah!" Flynn grinned amiably. "I was hoping you'd be at home."

He was carrying a package which was clearly a bottle of something.

"Where's Grover?" Fletch asked, coming into the hall.

He took Flynn's outstretched hand.

"I have some time of my own, you know," Flynn said. "The department lets me off the leash sometimes on the weekend. Had to come near by—wanted to pick up a Schönberg score the store doesn't have in yet—and happened to consider the City of Boston owes you a bottle of whisky."

He presented his package with the full joy of giving.

"That's damned nice of you."

It was twelve-year-old Pinch.

"Hope I'm not disturbing anything?"

"Oh, no. I was just going to see a couple of Alec Guinness pictures at the Exeter Street Theatre. That's near by, isn't it?"

"What a darling man! He's Irish, you know. Most English people you think of with talent are." He rubbed his hands together. "I thought it being a rainy Saturday afternoon, you might like to sit with me over a taste . . .?"

"I thought you never touch the stuff?"

"I never do. But, like work itself, I never mind watching another man partake." He turned to Mrs. Sawyer. "I don't suppose you keep a camomile tea?"

She said, "I think we've got Red Zinger."

"Any herb tea will do. Perhaps you'd bring a glass, some ice and water into the study as well, for Mister Fletcher here."

The thing seemed decided.

Flynn stepped into the den.

Fletch snapped on the lights and began to open the odd-shaped bottle.

Flynn rummaged around inside his sweater, having driven his hand through the neck of it, and pulled two sheets of folded paper from his shirt pocket.

"I was able to secure the complete passenger list for Flight 529 from Rome last Tuesday." He handed it to Fletch, who put down the open bottle. "I wonder if you'd cast your eye along that and see if there are any names you know."

"You think Ruth Fryer's murder might have something to do with something I was doing in Rome, eh?"

"Mister Fletcher, you said yourself, people hate you all over the world. Surely, one might spend an airfare to wreak your undoing."

Most of the names on the list were Italian; most of the rest were Irish—modern-day pilgrims on a flight between Rome and America in search of spiritual consolation or material attainment.

Flynn stood, hands in his pockets, chin back, the amiable grin still on his face.

"Supposing we were friends, Mister Fletcher," he said. "What would I call you? Surely not Irwin Maurice. Are you used to the name Peter, yet? Or are you down to calling yourself 'Pete'?"

"Fletch," Fletch said. "People call me Fletch."

"Fletch, is it? Now that's an impudent enough name. Couldn't an Irish poet dance a Maypole playing with a name like that, though?"

"I recognize no one's name on the list."

Fletch handed it back to him.

"I was afraid you'd say that."

"And I should call you Francis Xavier, right?"

"People call me Frank," said Flynn. "Except my wife, who calls me Frannie. She has a kindlier, softer view of me."

Mrs. Sawyer entered with a tray.

"I had the hot water on, anyway," she said.

On the tray were an ice bucket, an empty glass, a water carafe, a teapot, cream, sugar, a cup, saucer, spoon.

"Ah, that's lovely." Flynn rubbed his hands again. "Tell me, Mrs. Sawyer, when you left here after cleaning up Monday night, was there water in the carafe in the living room next to the whisky bottle?"

"No, sir. Of course, there wasn't. That had been washed out, dried out, and stoppered."

"I wouldn't think so. Who'd leave water out to go stale, when it's so easily replaceable? Was the whisky bottle there when you left?"

"What whisky bottle? Which whisky bottle?"

"There was more than one?"

"There were a lot of bottles on that table. That was Mister Connors' little bar. There were Scotch bottles, bourbon bottles, gin bottles, sherry and port decanters. Plenty of clean glasses."

"What happened to them?"

"Mister Fletcher put them away. I found them all in a cupboard in the kitchen. I figured he couldn't stand the sight of such things anymore than I can."

Flynn looked his question at Fletch.

"No," Fletch said. "I didn't."

"And," Flynn asked Mrs. Sawyer, "I suppose you've been rummaging around in that cupboard, touching the bottles and thus obliterating any fingerprints which might have been on them?"

"Of course I've been touching the bottles. I've been shoving them back and forth. They've been in the way of the sugar, salt and pepper."

" 'The sugar, salt and pepper.' A most active cupboard. No use," said Flynn. "Thank you, Mrs. Sawyer."

"You want anything else, you just let me know," she said.

"I'm so far behind in my own work, I have no hope of finishing anyway."

"Salt of the earth," said Flynn, pouring out his tea. "Salt of the earth." Across the hall, the kitchen door swung shut. "Of course it's always the salt of the earth that destroys the evidence."

They sat in the red leather chairs, two men in sweaters, one in a jacket as well, one with a cup of tea, the other with a Scotch and water.

Through the light curtains of the long windows was a dark sky. Every few moments a gust of wind from the Boston Gardens splattered a sheet of rain against the windows.

From six storeys below they could hear the hiss of tyres going along Beacon Street.

"A dark, gloomy day like this," said Flynn, "reminds me of when I was a boy in Munich, growing up. Dark days, indeed."

"Munich?"

"Let's see. On a day like this, a rainy fall Saturday afternoon, I'd be obliged to be in the gymnasium—the real gymnasium, the sports place—doing push-ups, scrambling up ropes, wrestling until the blood was ready to burst our heads."

"You're Irish."

"That I am. Or we'd be out running miles in the wet, around the countryside, looking out for the little red markers, sweat and rain mixed on our faces, the air heavy in our lungs, the ground just turning hard beneath our feet. What a splendid way to bring a boy up. No doubt I owe my current hardy constitution to it."

"To what?"

"I was a member of the Hitler Youth."

"You what?"

"Ah, yes, laddy. A man is many things, in his past."

"The *Jugendfuehrer?*"

"You've got it just right, laddy."

"How is that possible?"

"As you've said yourself : anything is possible. It this whisky all right?"

"Very good," said Fletch.

"Not being a drinking man myself, I'm shy in making choices for others. I'm afraid it was the peculiar shape of the bottle that caught my eye."

"It's fine."

"I don't suppose one should buy the whisky for the bottle?"

"One might as well."

"For all you drink, you mean. I see you're not a gulper."

"Not in front of you, anyway. How could Francis Xavier Flynn be a member of the *Jugendfuehrer?*"

"Now, haven't I asked myself that same question a thousand times?"

"I've just asked you again."

"The Republic of Ireland, of course, had little to do with the war. Relentlessly neutral, as they say, on the side of the Allies. My Da was the Republic's consul to Munich. Is it getting clearer?"

"No."

"In 1938, when I was about seven years old, it was decided, because of the unusual world circumstances, that I would stay on in Munich with my parents, instead of returning home to school by myself, as would have been normal. I spoke German as well as any boy my age, had had my first years in German schools, looked and dressed German. And, as my Da said, entrusting me with this great responsibility, I had reached the Age of Reason.

"So my Da took up agreein' with the Nazis in public, although he hated their ideas as any decent man would. We remained in Germany throughout the war. I remained in the German school, became a member of the Hitler Youth. The short pants, the neckerchief, the salute, the whole thing. Marched in the rallies. Was the young star at some of the gymnastic shows. People forgot I was Irish altogether."

"Flynn, really...."

"Believe it, if you will. I was a perfect member of *Jugendfuehrer.*

"But, you know, you'd be surprised what a wee boy in short pants and a Hitler Youth shirt and a bicycle and a camera can do. He can roam the countryside, sometimes with his friends. Tours of installations would be set up for us. You'd be amazed how soldiers and officers will show things to a wee boy they wouldn't show their own mothers. Anything I didn't understand, I'd take a picture of; anytime I came across what I suspected was a Nazi dignitary, I'd get his autograph. You'd be surprised at the number of high Nazi officers who'd be moving about in great secrecy but would stop to sign their names on a slip of paper for a small boy. Ah, I was a wonder, I was.

"And I had a couple of friends I corresponded with all during these years, in Dublin. One was Timmy O'Brien, Master

Timothy O'Brien, and the other was Master William Cavanaugh. I used to write them excited letters about my life, where I'd been and what I'd seen. I was full of the old Nazi malarkey—a bragging schoolboy, I was, if you read the letters. Sometimes I'd get letters back, doubting my word. I'd send photographs and autographs, and every proof I had.

"Of course, my Da was the ghostwriter of my side of the correspondence. And both Masters O'Brien and Cavanaugh had their actual address in London, at headquarters for British Intelligence."

"My God."

"An unusual way to grow up. My father also was using the consulate to help sneak British and American fliers out of the country, home again. It was all very difficult on my mother."

"Is this true, Flynn?"

"I was fourteen at the end of the war. Munich was rubble. There was no food to be had. I expect you've seen the pictures. It's all true.

"Before the Nazis withdrew, they shot my parents. Each of them. A single bullet between the eyes. In the kitchen of our apartment. I don't think the Nazis had any evidence against them. I think it was one of those arbitrary murders. There were lots of such incidents, those days. I found them after standing an air raid watch."

"What did you do then?"

"Oh, there were weeks and months to go yet. At first, I lived with the family of a friend. They didn't have any food or heat, either. I was on the street, living under things that had already fallen down. Even after the surrender, there were weeks and weeks of wandering around. You see, I was afraid to go up to the British or American soldiers. An odd thing. I was afraid of them. Of course, I was half-crazy.

"One night, sleeping in an alley, I got the toe of a boot in my ribs. Someone spoke to me in the lilt. A soldier was standing over me. You can believe he got an earful of Irish like he'd never had!

"Then it was home for me, back to Dublin. I was put in a Jesuit seminary, if you'd believe it. I guess it was my choice. I'd seen hell, you see.

"I learned another logic, got my health back. By the age of twenty I was tired of truth. Can you understand that?"

"Of course."

"The celibacy had worn thin, too. So I wrote a friend of mine, Master William Cavanaugh, in London. I sent the letter direct this time. Asking for a job. I gather the letter caused a great laugh, among the old boys.

"The rest of my life is a blank."

"I know you didn't work in Chicago."

"I know you know that. You did work in Chicago. What were you doing at the newspaper the other day, if you weren't enquiring about me?"

"You became a spy again."

"Did I say that?"

"But you married and had kids."

"I did that. An unusual thing for a lad who thought he'd be a priest to do."

"Odd for a spy, too."

"I wouldn't say that, precisely."

"Are you Catholic now?"

"Are the Catholics Catholic now, I'd want to know. My kids enjoy something or other, but what it is, I don't know. They disappear on the Sundays with their guitars and violins and bang around in some church, shaking hands and kissing each other. They tell me it's very exhilarating."

"Your wife is Irish? American? What?"

"She's from Palestine, a Jewish girl. I had a job of work to do out there in that area at one time. Would you believe we had to go to Fada to be married when she was pregnant? Neutral territory."

"Flynn, your being a Boston policeman is a cover. It's your cover."

"Why don't you pour yourself some fresh whisky, lad?"

"That's why you've said you have no experience as a policeman. You've never actually been a policeman."

"I have to bumble along," said Flynn. "Bumble along."

"You became a Boston policeman just at the time the intelligence agencies were being investigated by Congress and everyone else throughout the world."

"Have I said too much?" Flynn's face was a study in innocence. "It must be the tea talking."

"Can you still speak German?"

"In a way, it's my natural tongue."

"As a member of the Hitler Youth, did you ever actually have to pick up a gun and use it?"

"I did, yes."

"What happened?"

"In my confusion, I almost shot myself. I couldn't shoot at the Allied troops advancing on Munich. I couldn't shoot the lads I had been brought up with."

"What did you do?"

"I cried. I lay down in a ditch of mud and I cried. I wasn't fifteen yet, lad. I doubt I'd do anything different today."

A heavy gust blew a sheet of rain against the windows.

"Now it's your turn, Fletch."

XXIV

FLETCH mixed himself a second drink.

He said, "I doubt I have anything to say."

Even through the thick walls of the building they could hear the wind.

"I've done this much on you," said Flynn, from his chair. "Born and raised in Seattle. You have Bachelor's and Master's degrees from Northwestern. You didn't complete your Ph.D."

"The money ran out."

Fletch sat down again in his chair.

"You concentrated in journalism and fine arts. You wrote on the arts for a newspaper in Seattle. Broke a story there regarding the illicit importing of pre-Columbian Canadian objects. You joined the Marine Corps, were sent to the Far East, and won the Bronze Star, which you have never accepted. You then worked as an investigative reporter for the *Chicago Post*. You broke several big stories there, as you did later for a newspaper in California. As an investigative reporter—not as a critic."

"There's a difference?"

"About eighteen months ago, you disappeared from southern California."

"It's hard to get full co-operation from a newspaper these days," said Fletch. "One doesn't get to be a newspaper executive without political savvy—which is utterly destructive to the newspaper."

"You've been married and divorced twice, and there has been

a continuous flap in the courts about your refusal to pay alimony. Charges against you, from fraud to contempt—all, I suspect, incurred in your line of duty—were all dropped. Incidentally, after enquiring about you through several California police agencies, I received a personal phone call from the district attorney, or assistant district attorney, somewhere out there, a Mister Chambers, I think he said his name was, giving you high marks for past co-operation in one or two criminal cases."

"Alston Chambers. We were in the Marines together."

"Where have you been the last eighteen months?"

"Travelling. I was in Brazil for a while. The British West Indies. London. I've been living in Italy."

"You returned to this country once, to Seattle, for your father's funeral. Did you say you inherited your money from him?"

"No. I didn't say that."

"He was a compulsive gambler," Flynn said.

Fletch said, "I know."

"You didn't answer the question as to where your money came from."

"An old uncle," Fletch lied. "Died while I was in California."

"I see." Flynn accepted the lie as a lie.

"He couldn't leave his money to my father, could he?"

"So there are a good many people in your past who'd like to do you harm," Flynn said. "That's the trouble with crime in a mobile society. People wander all over the face of the earth, dragging their pasts with them. A good investigation these days is almost completely beyond a local police department, no matter how good."

"Your tea must be getting cold," Fletch said.

"Just as good cold as hot." Flynn poured himself some more. "We Europeans aren't as sensitive to temperature as you Americans are."

Fletch said, "You're thinking my past may have caught up with me in some way. Someone has followed me here and purposely put me in this pickle."

"Well, I'd hate to have to fill up the other side of the page that contains the list of your enemies. Isn't it said that a good journalist has no friends?"

"I think you're wrong, Inspector. As Peter Fletcher I was the victim of an accidental frame-up. Someone committed murder in this apartment and arranged things to hang the blame on the next person coming through the front door."

"Take this Rome situation, for example," said Flynn. "Can you explain it to me?"

"What do you mean?"

"Well, now, I not only observe what a man does do, but what he doesn't do, if you take my meaning. You told me the other night that you're here to do research into the life of the painter Edgar Arthur Tharp, Junior, the pinto painter, for a biography."

"That's right."

"Yet, since Wednesday morning, mind you, until last night, you had not been in touch with either the Tharp Family Foundation, or the proper curator at the Boston Museum of Fine Arts."

Fletch said, "I've been busy."

"In fact, you haven't been. Our boyos watching you say you lead the life of a proper Boston old lady. Lunch at Locke-Ober's, then drinks at the Ritz. You spent a couple of hours in the offices of the *Boston Star*. Otherwise, you've been at home here, in someone else's apartment."

"I guess that's true, too."

"Do you sleep a lot, Mister Fletcher?"

"I've been putting together my notes."

"Surely you would have done that in the sunny climate of Italy before you came here."

"Well, I didn't."

"Except for Wednesday, of course. We don't know what you did on Wednesday. That was the day you slipped in one door and out the other at the Ritz-Carlton. Innocent as a honeybee, of course. That was before we knew we were on to a retired investigative reporter who has an innocent instinct for losing his tail. All we know is that you did not go to either the Museum or the Tharp Foundation Wednesday."

"You've got to understand, Inspector. I had been travelling. Jet lag. The shock of the murder. Realizing I was a suspect. I guess I just can't account for myself."

"Indeed?" Before the curtains and the leaden sky, the green eyes could have been cosmic lights. "You're engaged to be married to Angela de Grassi."

"You're good at names."

"I've lived many places. Now who is she?"

"She's a girl. An Italian girl. Daughter of Count de Grassi."

"Count de Grassi?"

"Count Clementi Arbogastes de Grassi."

"Is that the gentleman who died last week?"

"We think so."

" 'We think so !' What sort of an answer is that?"

"He's dead."

"You said you attended a 'sort of funeral'."

"Did I?"

"You did."

"I guess I did."

"Fletch, why don't you tell me the truth, straight out, instead of making me work like a dentist pulling teeth. It's my day off, you know."

"And you paid for the whisky yourself?"

"I did. And you might start by telling me why you're really here in Boston."

"Okay. I'm here looking for some paintings."

"Ah! That's the boy. Flynn finally gets to hear the story. Don't stint yourself, now. Be as expansive as you like."

"Andy de Grassi and I are engaged to be married."

"A blissful state. Does the young lady speak English?"

"Perfectly. She went to school in Switzerland and for a while here in this country."

"Very important to have a common language between a husband and wife, when it comes to arguing."

"A collection of paintings was stolen from her father's house, outside Livorno, a couple of years ago. Very valuable paintings."

"How many?"

"Nineteen objects, including one Degas horse."

"A Degas horse, you say? Bless my nose. And what would you say these nineteen objects are worth, taken all in all?"

"Hard to say. Possibly ten million, twelve million."

"Dollars?"

"Yes."

"By God, I knew I shouldn't have taken up the viola. Is it a rich family, the de Grassis?"

"No."

"Of course, you'd say that, being rich yourself."

"Andy was up in the villa with me, at Cagna."

"Enjoying premarital bliss."

"You love a story, don't you, Flynn?"

"Show me an Irishman who doesn't!"

"Your years in the Hitler Youth did you no harm that way."

"Made me hungrier for a good story."

"I get catalogues from around the world," Fletch said. "You

know what catalogues are, in the art world? They're published by museums of their collections, or of special shows. Dealers put them out as a means of offering what they have to sell, or, frequently, as it works out, what they have sold."

"I see. I think I knew that."

"One day Andy is going through a particular catalogue issued by a gallery here in Boston, the Horan Gallery."

"I've never heard of it."

"It's on Newbury Street."

"It would be."

"She recognizes one of the de Grassi paintings—a Bellini—sold."

"This is two years after the robbery?"

"About that."

"She shows me, and together we go through earlier Horan catalogues. Two issues back, there's another de Grassi painting—a Perugino—also sold."

"And this is the first you'd heard of the paintings since the robbery?"

"Yes."

"They show up for sale in Boston."

"It might be more accurate to say, they show up sold through Boston."

"I've got you."

"Andy's very excited. We pack our bags, jump into the car, and head for Livorno."

"Where the Count is. Is there a Countess?"

"I'm afraid so. But she's not Andy's mother."

"You're not too keen on her."

"Oh, she's all right, I suppose. Andy's not too high on her."

"Understandable."

"We were going to show the Count the two catalogues from the Horan Gallery."

"You didn't call ahead?"

"We were too excited, I guess. We came off the beach, changed, packed, jumped into the car. I don't think we even showered."

"Must have been an itchy ride."

"It was."

"You said you were 'going to show' the catalogues to the Count?"

"On the way down to Livorno, we hear on the car radio that Count Clementi Arbogastes de Grassi has been kidnapped."

"Kidnapped? My God. That's gotten to be altogether too popular a crime."

"Andy begins screaming. I drive even faster. We stop for cognac. I go like hell again. She stops to phone ahead. It was quite a ride."

"You got there."

"Usual kidnap story. Except that the ransom demand was for something over four million dollars."

"Good heavens."

"And the de Grassis are broke. After the paintings were gone, they had nothing. They had not been insured. The de Grassi *palazzo* outside Livorno is just a weedy, run-down old place. No land. Two old servants who are virtually retired."

"You said she had an apartment in Rome. How did they live?"

"The three of them, the Count, the Countess and Andy, had been living off an annuity which comes to about fifty thousand dollars a year."

"Not precisely broke."

"Not up to paying a four million dollar ransom."

"And you couldn't pay it yourself? I mean, from what your uncle left you."

"No way."

"I mean, this being your prospective father-in-law and all."

"Absolutely not. I couldn't do it. The de Grassi family has been inactive for decades now. They had no credit."

"So?"

"So we published statements, saying such a ransom was impossible. We received more messages, saying, essentially, pay up in full, or we murder him. I talked the ladies into publishing an audited accounting of the family's worth. The annuity, incidentally, is absolutely frozen. There was no way even that capital could be turned to cash. In Italian law, you see, the family is still more important than any individual in the family, including the head of the family."

"The Italians are famous for sticking together," said Flynn, "even at the sacrifice of one of them."

"Just more messages. Pay up or we murder. In five days. A week went by. Silence. Two weeks. Three weeks. We heard nothing more."

"So he was murdered?"

"So the Italian police believe."

"How long ago was this?"

"More than a month now. The authorities advised the de Grassis to put the matter out of their minds. To accept the fact the Count was dead. 'He could be buried anywhere in Italy, or off its shores', was their exact phrase. We had a memorial service for him last Monday."

"The 'sort of funeral'."

"The sort of funeral. It seemed real enough."

"So you, an ex-investigative reporter of some repute, decide to take matters into your own hands and come here to Boston to see what you can find out."

"That's about it."

"Have you talked with this man Horan?"

"Yes. Wednesday."

"That's where you were Wednesday."

"Yes."

"Then, of course, you went in one door of the Ritz-Carlton and out the Newbury Street door. The gallery is on Newbury Street!"

"Yes."

"By God, the man is relentlessly innocent. And does the man Horan have the rest of the paintings?"

"A dealer doesn't have paintings, Frank. He deals in them. The trick was to find out the source of the two de Grassi paintings he had already sold. His reputation checks out as clean as a whistle."

"I suppose you went about it in your usual direct manner."

"Difficult being direct with an art dealer, Frank. I asked him to find another painting for me. Another painting on the de Grassi list. A Picasso named 'Vino, Viola, Mademoiselle'."

"Did he turn it up?"

"After a few days, yesterday, he told me it belongs to a man in Dallas, Texas. He also says he has bought a couple of other paintings from this same man, within the last year or two. I mean, he has sold them for him, through his gallery."

"You have the Texan's name?"

"I have."

"And tell me, Fletch, to whom do these paintings belong, if you do find them?"

"That's the question. Menti's estate can't be settled for years."

" 'Menti'?"

"The Count's. The will can't be read until the body is found. Or enough years to pass for him to be declared dead."

"So, after you find the paintings, you have to find the body."

"No way I can do that. If the Italian police can't."

"No one knows whether the paintings belong to the daughter, or the widow?"

"No. What makes it worse is that until Menti's body is found, they don't even have an income."

"I daresay both ladies have eyes only for you at the moment."

"One would think so."

"Ach! And I thought your biggest problem at the moment was being a murder suspect."

"I suppose that's why I reacted so slowly at first to the idea I was a murder suspect."

"I knew you had a more-than-natural view of the murder, what with your calling the Police Business phone and all. If you had told me you once had been a reporter, I would have understood your professional reaction to a body in the living room a little better." Flynn shook the pot and poured himself a third cup of tea. "It's not every man who bounces blissfully from a kidnapping to a murder to another murder."

"Inured I think is the word."

"A good one, that."

"Do I understand, Inspector Francis Xavier Flynn, that you think there might be some connection between what went on in Italy—I mean, Menti's kidnapping and murder—and the murder of Ruth Fryer here?"

"I might."

"You had me check the airline's passenger list."

"There might be a connection, Irwin Maurice Fletcher, but at the moment I don't know what it is."

"There is a connection," said Fletch. "Someone did come from Rome with me."

"And who might that be?"

"The Countess. She flew through New York. She arrived in Boston Tuesday about an hour after I did."

"And did she know you were coming to this apartment?"

"She had my address and telephone number."

"She's hot after the paintings, is she?"

"Boiling after them."

"And how did she know you were looking for them?"

"I guess she read some notes I left Andy—my itinerary, that sort of thing. She knew I had a list of the paintings with me."

"But why would she kill Ruth Fryer?"

"Ruth may have been here in the apartment, naked, waiting to surprise Bart, not knowing he was in Italy. She opened the door to the Countess."

"The irate step-mother-in-law?"

"Well, damned angry and suspicious."

"Naturally, she thinks you're grabbing the paintings for Andy."

"Naturally."

"Are you?"

"Naturally."

"It's no good," said Flynn. "The bodice was torn."

"That could have happened any number of different ways. She could have done it herself, taking it off."

"Ruth Fryer didn't have a key to the apartment."

"But Joan Winslow does."

"The woman next door? She has a key? We forgot to ask that. Terrible thing, being an inspector of police inexperienced at the job. I should have asked. But why would she let Ruth Fryer in?"

"She probably wouldn't—if Joan were sober. She let me in."

"Did she, indeed? How very interesting. And where is the Countess now?"

"She moved in last night."

"Moved in here?"

"Yes. The Ritz-Carlton was too expensive."

"Ah! The Countess is the dish you had drinks with at the Ritz the other night. Ah, yes. The boyos were rather taken with her. And they said you didn't even pay the check!"

"I didn't."

"The Countess is rather cramping your style?"

"She'd like to."

"Well, well, now." Flynn gazed at the bottom of his empty teacup. "Haven't we learned a lot about each other?"

Fletch said nothing. His second drink was gone.

Flynn said, "I guess I should be shovin' home to my family."

The rain was still audible.

In the hall, Fletch asked, "How's the chubby City Council-person's murder coming?"

"It's not coming at all. Not at all. You'd think with such a murder, someone would step forward and take the credit, wouldn't you?"

"Thanks for the Scotch, Inspector."

Fletch pushed the elevator button.

Then he said, "Get me off the hook soon, will you, Frank?"

"I know. You want to go to Texas, trailing your entourage of women."

He went through the clunky elevator doors.

Descending the shaft, he said, his voice as quiet as always, "You're the best suspect I've got yet, Fletcher, no matter how you dance on the head of a pin. You might save me the bother by confessin'."

XXV

It was just past five o'clock in the afternoon, and Fletch was sleepy. The drinks with Flynn had unwound him.

He said good-night to Mrs. Sawyer, had a bowl of her stew, and, despite the hour, crawled into bed.

It was midnight, Rome time.

"Flesh, darling."

Someone was nibbling his ear.

A long, cool body pressed against his. A nipple grazed his forearm.

It was a fuller body than Angela's. Much.

A leg stroked the back of his own legs. Up and down.

"Sylvia!"

Even in the dark room, there was no mistaking the tousled hair of his step-mother-in-law-to-be against the pillow.

"Jesus Christ, Sylvia!"

"It's too late, darling."

She slipped her right hip under his.

"You read in the Bible, 'They knew each other in his sleep?'"

"This is incest!"

"So was that, darling."

She was fully under him, her hips moving.

Her breasts were back-breaking.

"God!"

It was too late.

There was only one thing he could do to prevent either one part of his body, or another, from breaking.

"It was not incest, darling."

118

Flat on his back, finally, Fletch read the luminous dial of his wristwatch. It was only eight o'clock at night.

"Did you have something to eat?" he asked.

"Of course," she said. "You expect me to put up with your tricks forever?"

"You've got some pretty good tricks of your own, Countess del Gassey."

"Where did you go last night? One, two hours I wait for my dinner."

"I went out."

"I know that. Son of a bitch." She sat up. "That's what you do! You tell me some crazy story and then you leave me with nothing! You're no grand chef! You're son of a bitch! You'll do the same thing with the paintings—tell me lies, lies! Leave me with nothing!"

He put his hand on her back.

"I left the front door unlocked for you. Did you get a nice man to let you in downstairs?"

"I had to wait, and wait. You didn't answer the buzzer."

"I was asleep."

Sitting up in the bed, in the dark, the Countess de Grassi began to cry.

"Oh, Flesh! You will help me."

"I will?"

"You have to help me!"

"I do?"

"Menti's dead. I'm an early widow. With nothing. Nothing!"

"Yeah."

"I have nothing, Flesh."

"Actually, you have a few things going for you."

"Angela's young, and she's pretty. Clever. She has her whole life ahead of her. Me? I have nothing."

"She's a de Grassi, Sylvia."

"Me? I'm the Countess de Grassi!"

"I've heard."

"I married Menti."

"And his paintings."

"They are my paintings. Menti would want me to have them. I know this. Many times he spoke of 'our paintings'."

"Sylvia, will you listen? Whose paintings they are is not for me to say. Either Menti mentioned them in his will, or he didn't. If he did mention them, they go to you, Andy, both of you, neither of you—whatever he directed in his will. If he didn't mention them, then it is for the Italian courts to decide—if we ever recover the paintings, that is."

She crawled inside his arm, snuggled next to him.

Fletch remembered seeing, on the beach at Cagna, her toes, with the nails polished.

She said, "If the paintings are in this country, then, how do you say, possession is the first law of nature."

"Self-preservation is the first law of nature, Sylvia—an instinct you have fully developed."

"I mean, possession."

"I know what you mean."

"Flesh, tell me the truth. You know where the paintings are."

"Sylvia, I am in Boston working on a biography of Edgar Arthur Tharp, Junior."

She slapped him lightly on the chest.

"You lie. All the time you lie to me."

"I am."

"You writing on such a big book, then where the typewriter? Where the papers? I looked all over the apartment last night. Nobody's writing a book here."

"I haven't started yet. I've had distractions."

" 'Distractions!' You find the paintings." He could feel breath from each nostril going against his side. "Where are the paintings?"

He was awake. And he was beginning to want it.

He said nothing.

She placed the side of her knee over his crotch and moved it. She said, "Where are the paintings? Eh, Flesh?"

"You're a hell of a negotiator, Sylvia."

"You will help me, Flesh. Won't you?"

"You help me first."

"America!" Fletch shouted.

It was at the worst possible moment that the telephone rang.

It was a cable. From Andy. Angela de Grassi.

"ARRIVING BOSTON SUNDAY SIX-THIRTY P.M. TWA FLIGHT 5.40. IS SYLVIA WITH YOU. MUCH LOVE.—ANDY."

Fletch said, "Oh, shit."

She never could keep herself to ten words or less.

He said, "Oh, Christ."

He said, "What, in hell, am I doing?"

Sylvia, "Come on, Flesh."

He said, "All right."

It was a somewhat better moment the next time the telephone rang.

Fletch said, "Hello?"

"Are you drunk?"

It was Jack Saunders. Fletch could hear the city room clatter behind him.

"No."

"Were you asleep?"

"No."

"What are you doing?"

"None of your fucking business."

"I've got it. Are you about through?"

"Buzz off, will you, Jack?"

"Wait a minute, Fletch. I'm stuck."

"So am I."

"Really stuck. Will you listen a minute?"

"No."

"Fires are breaking out all over Charlestown. A torch is at work. I haven't got the rewrite man I need."

"So?"

"One is drunk and ready for the tank. The other one is pregnant and just left for the hospital to have a baby. Nothing I can do about it. I can't find the day guy. His wife says he's at a ball-game somewhere. I'm three short on the desk, two with vacations and one with the 'flu. The guy I've got on rewrite now is a kid; he's not good enough for a big story like this."

"Sounds like very poor organization, Jack."

"Jeez, who'd think all hell would break loose on an October Saturday night?"

"I would."

"Can you come in?"

"For rewrite?"

"Yeah."

"You're crazy."

"I can't handle it myself, Fletch. I've got to remake the whole paper."

"What time is it?"

"Ten minutes to nine."

"What time do you go to bed?"

"We'll front-page big cuts for the first edition which goes at ten-twenty."

"Jack, I'm a murder suspect."

"Ralph Locke isn't."

"I don't know the city."

"You know how to put words together."

"I'm rusty."

"Please, Fletch? Old times' sake? I can't talk much longer."

Fletch looked through the dark at Sylvia, now on his side of the bed.

"I'll be right there. Bastard."

XXVI

"Frank?"

"Who do you want?"

The young voice was sleepy.

It was two-twenty-five Sunday morning.

"Inspector Flynn."

The telephone receiver clattered against wood.

At a distance from the phone, the voice said, "Da'?"

After a long moment, Flynn answered.

"Now who might this be?"

"I. M. Fletcher."

"God bless my nose. Where are you, lad? Would you be seizing upon this odd hour of the night to confess?"

"I'm at the *Star*, Frank."

"Now what would you be doing there? Have you rejoined the enemy?"

"Charlestown is on fire. Someone is torching it."

"I see."

"An old friend from the *Chicago Post* asked me to come in and help out."

"You have an old friend in Boston?"

"I guess so."

"Where was he the Tuesday last? Did you ask?"

"I know he has Monday and Tuesday nights off."

"No matter how much you talk to a man, ply him with drink, there's always more to learn."

"Frank, could I make this call quick?"

"You didn't have to make it at all."

"I'm sorry to wake you up."

"It's all right, lad. I was just filling in my time by sleeping, anyway."

"I can't get your Boston Police spokesman to listen to me."

"And who's speaking for us tonight?"

"A Captain Holman."

"Ach, he's a police spokesman, all right. That's precisely what he is."

"He calls every fifteen minutes with new facts, but I can't get him to listen."

"That's what a spokesman is: a person with two mouths and one ear, a freak of nature. What would you like to say to him?"

"I've got some facts, too. We've got more reporters in the field than you have bulls."

" 'We' now, is it? An inveterate journalist, I do believe is Mister I. M. Fletcher."

"Listen, Frank. It's very simple. Eleven fires have been set since seven o'clock. Mostly tenements, a few warehouses, one church. Nothing consistent."

"All empty?"

"Yes."

"Then that's consistent."

"Right. At the third, fifth, seventh, eighth, and ninth fires, empty, two-gallon containers of Astro gasoline have been found. You know, the kind of containers a gas station sells you when you're out of gas on the road somewhere?"

"Yes."

"I've sent a reporter back to the other fires to see if he can spot Astro containers there, too."

"Haven't the Fire Department's arson boys caught on, yet?"

"No. They're doing the usual. Watching the spectators. They won't listen to the reporters who keep finding these containers. They're just taking pictures."

"I know their method. They'll have a meeting in the morning, to compare notes. It gives them something to do, with their coffee."

"The arsonist should be pinned tonight."

"I agree," said Flynn. "All that smoke is air polluting."

"All these fires are taking place around Farber Hill. All sides of it, more or less equally. First a fire starts on the north side, then one on the south side, then one on the north-west side."

"That could cause a terrific traffic jam of city equipment," Flynn said. "Collisions."

"I looked at a district map. In the geographic dead centre of the district, at the corner of Breed and Acorn streets, is a gas station."

"And you're going to tell me . . . ?"

"The map doesn't say which company runs the station, so I asked a reporter to drive over and look."

"Did he collide with anything?"

"It's an Astro station, Frank."

"So whom are we looking for?"

"A young gas station attendant, who works at the Astro station at the corner of Breed and Acorn streets, and who got off duty at six o'clock."

"Why young?"

"He's moving awfully fast, Frank. Over fences. In second-storey windows."

"So he must be agile, and therefore he is probably young. Quick in the knee, as it were."

"And he has access to a lot of Astro gasoline containers."

"All right, Fletch." Flynn's voice lowered. "I'll pull on my pants and wander over to Charlestown. See if I can help out. I have a natural dislike of seeing a city on fire, you know?"

"I know."

"Tell me, Fletcher. After we catch this arsonist boyo, will we also discover he's the murderer of Ruth Fryer?"

"Good night, Frank. If you get the guy, will you call the *Star*?"

"I'll see Captain Holman does."

"Ask him to talk to Jack Saunders."

"I'll do that. I'm always very co-operative with the press, you know."

XXVII

DRIVING through the light, Sunday mid-morning traffic in the Ghia, very considerate of the two policemen following him, Fletch easily found 58 Fenton Street in Brookline.

He had had four hours' sleep in one of his own guest rooms.

He had not renewed contact with the guest asleep in his own bed.

Lucy Connors opened the door of Apartment 42 to him.

Purposely, he supposed, she was dressed in a full peasant skirt and a light blouse with low neck and puffy sleeves. She wore no make-up, nor jewellery.

"Martin Head?"

"Yeah," Fletch said. *"Très Magazine."*

Lucy's eyes went from one of his empty hands to the other, possibly checking for a camera or a tape recorder.

"Good of you to see me," he said. "Especially on a Sunday morning."

"I wouldn't dare have you come any other time. It might improve my reputation."

The apartment was the usual one or two bedroom arrangement. A small dining table was in a corner of the living room. Along the wall next to it was a hi-fi rig, with album-filled shelves.

There was a cheap, old divan along the opposite wall, an undersized braided rug in front of it, a saggy upholstered chair to one side.

A drapeless window ran along the fourth wall, letting in a harsh light.

The only wall decoration in the room was a Renoir print over the divan.

"Marsha?" Lucy said.

That was the introduction.

Marsha Hauptmann was stretched out like a board, her slim haunches in the far corner of the divan, the heels of her moccasin topsiders on the floor in front of her, hands in the pockets of her blue jeans. She wore a heavy, blue naval shirt, opened at the throat, sleeves rolled above the elbows.

Her hair was a perfect black, shining pageboy, her skin as translucent as a well-scrubbed child's.

She did not move her head, nor her body, as Fletch entered.

Her dark eyes moved into his, seeing nothing else, expressing more curiosity and challenge than hostility.

Fletch said, "Marsha."

"Would you like some coffee, Martin?"

Clearly, Lucy was nervous. Her new way of life was about to be questioned by a detached professional.

"Not unless you're having some."

"We aren't," said Lucy.

She sat on the divan, a full seat away from Marsha.

Fletch sat in the chair.

"I'm glad you're doing this, Lucy," he said. "People need to understand what you've been through."

"No one has understood," she said. "Not my family, friends. Not Bart. I rather thought Bart might understand, or I wouldn't have been so frank with him. He took it as some kind of a personal insult."

She gave Marsha's forearm a tug, pulling her hand out of her pocket. She held Marsha's hand. "Really, Martin, it's a matter of complete indifference to me as to who understands and who doesn't."

"Of course." He coughed quickly. "You've solved your problems. Others haven't."

Marsha's eyes warmed towards him.

"I'm afraid most people think this is the problem," Lucy said. "I mean, Marsha and I living together. Like it's acne or the 'flu or something that will go away." She gave Marsha's hand a self-conscious squeeze. "I guess I went through that phase, too. But why are you more interested in me than in Marsha?"

"I'm interested in Marsha, too," said Fletch. "But you're a little older. You were married. I would guess you gave up quite a lot, in the way of material things, to live with Marsha. I would think you have had to make the bigger adjustments."

"I guess so. Marsha's lucky. She's always been a little dyke." She smiled fondly at Marsha. "Straight through school. All those shower rooms after field hockey, eh, Marsha?" To Fletch, she said, "Marsha went to boarding school, a much better education than I had. Self-discovery. She started sleeping with girls when she was about twelve."

Marsha remained silent, a lanky love object at the end of the divan.

"I had to go through the whole thing," Lucy said. "Boy, was I thick."

"Tell me about it." Fletch took notebook and pen from his pocket. "Tell me about 'the whole thing'."

"As 'Mrs. C?' "

"Absolutely."

"And I get to see the manuscript before you hand it in?"

"Absolutely."

"Okay." She exhaled. "Shit." Still holding on to her hand, she glanced at Marsha. "You know. A nice girl. Brought up. Goals set for me. A role set for me. We lived in Westwood, a lawn in front, a lawn in back, a two-car garage. Dad owned an automobile agency. My mother was neurotic, a pill freak. Still is. I hated Jack, my older brother. He was plain, simply cruel. Big hockey player. I mean, when Mother was freaked out, he'd stick pins in the hamster. He'd stick pins in anything. I barely survived him. Bastard."

Marsha's eyes rolled to study Lucy's face worriedly.

"I was considered good-looking," Lucy said hesitantly. "You know what that means in an American public high school. First one in a training bra, first one to wear falsies, first one to bleach my hair—at thirteen. First one to beat the baby fat off my ass. Goal-oriented. Cheerleader. Little skirts and pompoms. First one to get laid. Very goal-oriented. I didn't enjoy it. Getting laid, I mean. But it was a goal. The first guy to lay me, the full-back, must have weighed two hundred and twenty pounds. A fat, grey belly. It was not fun. Damned near broke me in two.

"I went to junior college. Went with a guy from Babson who played the violin and was full of the secret international commodity cartel he was going to run. A real drip.

"At a party I met Bart. I was getting near graduation. Bart was a goal. He looked normal, acted normal. Dartmouth College, Harvard Law. Going a little bald. Older than I was by twelve years. In a law firm. Very rich. I played innocent and let him thrill me. I was very dishonest, but people are, sometimes, in attaining their goals."

Fletch asked, "Did you have any sexual feeling for him at all?"

"How did I know? I didn't know what sexual feeling was. Look, I had been told boys turn girls on and girls turn boys on and that was it. There was nothing else. Whatever happened between me and a boy I figured I was turned on."

"But you weren't."

"No way."

"Never?"

Firmly, she said, "Never. I hear some are, but not me—ever. It was pure role-playing. I played the game with myself, 'someday my crisis will come'. I wasn't even excited. Only I didn't even know it."

"Come on, Lucy," Fletch said. "You knew such a thing as lesbianism existed."

"No, I didn't. It never entered my head. I mean, I knew such a thing existed. Creatures like Marsha. Way over there, somewhere. Far out. They were different. Really weird. I mean, I didn't relate to them at all. I was very successful at suppressing my own, real sexual nature. Totally successful."

"Okay," Fletch said.

"Soon after we were married, Bart started asking me about frigidity. Conversationally, you know? What did I know about it? He began having these long talks with the woman in the next apartment, and then coming to bed stinko. When he was on trips out of town, I picked up a guy or two. For Bart's sake. Nothing ever happened. I mean, I never got turned on by anybody. So when he suggested a psychiatrist, I went along with it. He was beginning to make me think something was wrong.

"The psychiatrist was a great guy. He got me towards the truth very quickly. I turned him off, ran away from him. Ran away from the truth. It was just too shocking. You know, I was one of those creatures 'over there'. I like girls. I tried to bullshit the psychiatrist. He was a slob, but by then I was too close to the truth. I couldn't bullshit myself. I was listening to myself. This went on a long, long time. A terribly long time.

"I was bitchy, irascible, tough, mean, violent. Bart and I had slugging matches. I hit him. I threw things at him. I mean, I hit him with things, objects, anything at hand."

"You did?"

"Yes."

"I see."

"He had so many goddamned welts on his face, so often, he had to tell the people at the office he was doing boxing as a sport. He might as well have been living with a bad-tempered, second-string welterweight. I was really violent."

"Are you still?"

"No."

Marsha looked at her from beneath half-drawn lids.

"Well, I mean," Lucy said. "Sometimes we play. You know?"

"Yeah," said Fletch.

"I felt I was in some kind of a box, and had to fight my way out. Can you understand that, Martin?"

"Sure."

"It's a wonder I didn't belt a few shrinks along the way. I took everything out on poor old Bart."

"So how did you meet Marsha?" Fletch asked.

"One day I went into a boutique, and saw something I liked—Marsha. She waited on me. I bought a shirt. Next day I went back and bought a pair of pants. The third day I went in and started to buy a bikini. I called her into the dressing room to ask her how she thought it fitted me. I was feeling something. The tingle. I guess I was opened up enough then to the idea of girls. I had been forced to become conscious of my real desires. In the dressing room, Marsha put the palm of her hand against my hip, looked me in the eyes, and said, 'Who are you bullshitting?' " Lucy picked up Marsha's hand, and looked at it, wonderingly. "Her first touching me was the most satisfactory feeling I'd ever had."

They looked at each other, apparently recalling the moment.

Fletch looked at his notebook.

Finally, Lucy said, "Are you straight, Martin?"

"You mean, do I like girls?"

"Yes."

"Yes."

"I guess that's how you can understand."

Fletch chuckled. "I guess so."

"I mean, you don't seem offended."

"I'm not. Why should I be?"

"Would you be if I were your sister?"

"I don't think so."

"Some are."

"Everybody should be what he or she is."

Lucy said, "Bart even suggested religion for me. Jesus."

"How did you handle the marital situation?" Fletch asked.

"First, I went throught a long period thinking I could have it both ways. Marsha and I were making it together. Sometimes here. Sometimes at my place. It was beautiful. Too good. It was the real thing. It wasn't a passing phase on my part. It was me. We were getting careless. I mean, we were even doing it at my apartment while a servant was there. Oh, my God. I realized unconsciously, I wanted Bart to find out. He was too thick. I finally had to tell him."

Fletch asked, "How did he take it?"

"I said, like a personal insult. He thought he had enough masculinity for both of us. He thought he could snap me out of it, if I just gave myself to him fully. He suggested more psychiatrists. He suggested religion. He even suggested we go into a marriage-of-convenience thing, both of us making love to girls on the side. That was about the last straw. By then Marsha had come to mean just too much to me. As a person, you know?"

Again they exchanged looks. Marsha's hand was squeezed.

"Bart set up the boutique for us. Financially. I mean, the one we now run. You can forget the name of it. We don't need the publicity."

"Does he still own it?"

"He's still financing it. We're not completely divorced yet."

"You say he was hurt?"

"I guess so. I guess this revelation about me caused him to question his own masculinity. I mean, he loved me, he married me, and I wasn't there at all."

"But at the same time, apparently he hadn't found your sexual relations satisfactory."

"He had put up with them. He hadn't thrown me out. It might have been better if he had. Instead, he had tried to help."

"Do you ever see each other?"

"We bump into each other. Boston's a small city. Everybody's always embarrassed. These days, you know, everybody knows everybody else's sexual business."

"Hey, Marsha?" Fletch said. "What do you think?"

Lucy looked at her expectantly.

Bright, dark eyes in Fletch's, Marsha shook her head slightly, and said nothing.

Fletch closed his notebook and put it in his pocket.

"Again, sorry about coming on a Sunday morning," he said. "I tried several times to phone you Tuesday night. Weren't you here?"

"Tuesday?" Lucy looked puzzled at Marsha. "Oh, Tuesday. I was in Chicago, buying for the boutique. I was supposed to fly back Tuesday afternoon, but the plane was late. I was here by nine o'clock. You were here, weren't you, Marsha?"

She said, "Yeah."

"I have to fly out to Chicago sometime soon," Fletch said. "What did you fly, Pan American?"

"TWA," Lucy said.

"That's better, uh?"

"We were supposed to arrive at five, but it was seven-thirty before we got to Boston. Fog."

"Well, Lucy, I thank you very much. Will you keep the name of Connors?"

"I don't think so. I guess I'll use my maiden name. Hyslop. Get out of Bart's hair. What's left of it."

Looking straight at Fletch, Marsha said, "You didn't call here Tuesday night."

"I tried." Fletch stood up and put his pen in his inside jacket jocket. "Phone must have been out of order."

Marsha's eyes followed him as he went towards the door.

Lucy followed him.

Fletch said, "What's this about a murder in your husband's apartment?"

"That's irrelevant," said Lucy.

"I know. I'm just curious. I mean, murders are interesting."

"Not for the story?"

"Of course not. What's it got to do with you?"

"Some girl was murdered in our old apartment. After Bart left for Italy. He rented the apartment to some schnook who says he found the body."

"You mean, your husband killed her?"

"Bart? You're kidding. There's not an ounce of violence in him. Believe me, I should know. If he were going to kill anybody, he would have killed me."

"Have the police questioned you?"

"Why should they?"

From across the room, the harsh light from the window streaking between them, Marsha's eyes were locked on Fletch's face.

"You must still have a key to the apartment," he said.

"I suppose I do," she said. "Somewhere."

"Interesting," said Fletch.

"The police probably don't know where to find me," Lucy said. "Everything here is under Marsha's name. You wouldn't have known where to find me, if Bart hadn't given you the number."

"That's right."

"I'm still surprised he did. Bart must be coming to the idea that this situation happens to other people, too."

Fletch said, "Your husband's a surprising fellow."

"How did you happen to meet him?"

"He's doing some trust work for my editor. We all happened to be together in Montreal," Fletch said, "Tuesday night."

Marsha still had not moved. Her eyes, clear and unwavering,

remained on Fletch's face. A small amount of fear had entered those eyes.

"When will we see your story?" Lucy asked.

"Oh, a few weeks." Fletch opened the door. "I'll send it to you. If it works out."

XXVIII

T H E Countess was not at the apartment when Fletch returned.

She had left a note for him saying she had gone to mass.

When the downstairs door's buzzer rang, Fletch shouted into the mouthpiece, "Who is it?"

"Robinson."

It was certainly not the Countess's voice.

"Who?"

"Clay Robinson. Let me in."

Fletch had never heard of Clay Robinson.

He let him in.

Fletch stood in the opened front door, listening to the elevator.

A curly-haired man in his mid-twenties got off the elevator. His face was puffy, his eyes red-rimmed and bloodshot, the pupils glazed. His lips were cracked.

As soon as he let himself through the elevator doors, he returned his hands to the pockets of his raincoat.

"Fletcher?"

"Yeah?"

The man's words slurred.

"I was engaged to marry Ruth Fryer."

Fletch took a step forward with his left foot and swung with his right hand. His fist landed hard against Robinson's jaw.

Going down, Robinson couldn't get his hands out of his pockets.

He crashed against the small table under the mirror across from the elevator, rolled off it, and fell on to the floor, a flurry of raincoat.

Fletch put his right knee at the base of Robinson's rib cage and knelt hard on it.

In the right-hand pocket of the raincoat, inside Robinson's

hand, Fletch felt the pistol. Robinson's eyes rolled towards his brows.

Fletch grabbed the gun from the pocket and stood up. It was a .22 calibre target pistol.

Robinson sat on the rug, one arm straight to the floor, a knee up, his other hand gently touching his jaw.

"Come in," Fletch said.

He went into his apartment and put the gun in a drawer of the desk in the den.

When he returned to the apartment's foyer, Robinson was standing in the door, dazed, right hand in coat pocket, left hand rubbing his jaw.

"Come in," Fletch said.

He closed the door behind Robinson.

"I'll put some coffee on. You take a shower."

He walked Robinson down the corridor to the master bedroom's bathroom. Sylvia's things were everywhere.

"Hot, then cold."

Fletch left him in the bathroom.

He heard the shower running while he crossed the hall to the den with a coffee tray.

After a while Robinson appeared in the door of the den, hair wet, tie hanging from his opened collar, raincoat over his arm.

His eyes were less glazed.

"Have some coffee," Fletch said.

Robinson dropped his coat on a side chair, and sat in a red leather chair.

"You've had a rough time." Fletch handed him a cup of steaming, black coffee. "I'm sorry."

Robinson, saucer held at chest level, sipped his coffee, blinking slowly.

Fletch said, "I didn't kill Ruth Fryer. Nothing says you have to believe me, or even can believe me. I found her body. She was a beautiful girl. And she looked like a hell of a nice person. I didn't kill her."

Robinson said, "Shit."

"Shooting me would have been a real mistake," Fletch said. "But I dig the impulse."

In his chair, Robinson choked. Then, breath out of control, he put his coffee on the side table, his face forward in his hands, and sobbed.

Fletch went into the living room and studied the Paul Klee.

The noise from the den was a full-chested, strangulated, broken-hearted sobbing. It stopped. Then it started again.

When the pauses became more frequent, and longer, Fletch went back to the bathroom and soaked a hand towel in cold water. He wrung it out.

Going back into the den, he tossed the wet towel at Robinson. "Anything I can do for you?"

Robinson rubbed his face in the towel, then pushed it back over his hair.

He sat, head over his knees, towel pressed against his forehead.

"Were you at the funeral?" Fletch asked.

"Yes. Yesterday. In Florida."

"How are her parents?"

"There's only her father."

Fletch said, "I'm sorry for him. I'm sorry for you."

Clay Robinson sat back in a slouch.

"I hadn't broken down before this. I guess I've been holding myself pretty tight." He grinned. "The thought of killing you got me through it."

"Do you want some food?"

"No."

"And you don't want anything to drink."

"No."

"Where are you from?"

"Washington. I work for the Justice Department."

"Oh?"

"A clerk. A clerk with a college education."

"How did you meet Ruth Fryer?"

"On an airplane. I was flying some papers in from Los Angeles. We spent the night together."

"You picked her up."

"We met," said Clay Robinson. "Fell in love. We were getting married New Year's."

"I don't remember her wearing an engagement ring."

"I hadn't bought one yet. Have you ever lived on a clerk's pay?"

"Yes."

"I came up Tuesday," Clay said.

"To Boston?"

"Yes. I was going to surprise her. I knew she had ground duty all this week. I took some time off. By the time I got to the hotel, she had gone."

"Do you know with whom?"

"No. Her room-mate just said Ruth's uniform was there, so she must have changed and gone out. I didn't know about it, about the murder, until next morning when I went to the airport to find her."

"What did you do?"

"I don't know. I don't remember. It was the next morning I called her father and began to make arrangements to fly the body down. The police had already done an autopsy. Arrogant bastards."

"Where did you get the gun?"

"Pawn shop in the South End. Paid a hundred dollars for it."

"This morning?"

"Last night."

"Where did you stay last night?"

"Mostly in a bar. I got pretty drunk. I fell into some hotel at two, three this morning."

"Want some more coffee?"

"I don't know what I want."

"There's an unused guest room in there," Fletch said. "If you want to hit the bed, it's all right with me."

"No." A little more clear-eyed, Robinson looked at Fletch wonderingly. "I was going to kill you."

"Yeah."

"You moved mighty fast."

Fletch said, "What are you going to do now?"

"I'm going to find Ruthie's murderer."

"Good for you."

"What do you know about it?" Robinson asked. "I mean, about the murder."

"It's being handled by Inspector Francis Xavier Flynn of the Boston Police Department."

"Who does he think killed Ruthie?"

"Me."

"Who do you think killed Ruthie?"

"I have a couple of ideas."

"Are you going to tell me?"

"No."

Robinson said, "You have the gun."

"Yeah," Fletch said, "but you might have another hundred dollars."

Robinson's white face moved as slowly as changes in the moon.

"Why don't you go home?" Fletch said. "Go downstairs, get

into a taxi, go to the airport, take the next plane to Washington, taxi to your apartment, have something warm to eat, go to bed, and tomorrow morning go to work."

Robinson said, "Sounds nice."

"Thought it would if someone laid it out for you."

Robinson said, "All right."

He stood up stiffly and reached for his raincoat.

"What am I supposed to say to you?"

Fletch said, "Good-bye?"

"I guess if I ever find out you are the murderer, I will kill you."

"Okay."

"Even if they put you in jail for twenty, thirty years, however long, when they release you, I will kill you."

"It's a deal."

At the door, Robinson said, "Good-bye."

Fletch said, "Come again. When you're feeling better."

Before leaving the apartment himself, an hour or two later, Fletch wrote a note to the Countess saying he had gone to the airport to pick up Andy.

XXIX

I T W A S a dark brown, wooden Victorian house, three storeys under a slate roof, on the harbourside, in Winthrop. It had a small front yard and cement steps leading up to a deep porch.

Looking between the houses, as he walked from where he had parked his car, Fletch saw their shallow backyards ended at a concrete seawall. Beyond was the cold, slate-grey, dirty water of Boston Harbour. The airport was a mile or two across the water.

On the porch, Fletch looked through the front window, into the living room.

At the back of the room, four music stands were set up in a row. Behind them, to their right, was a baby grand piano, its lid piled with stacks of sheet music. A 'cello stood against the piano. The divan and chairs, coffee table, and carpet seemed incidental in the large, wainscoted room.

Two teenage boys who looked just alike, not only in their blue jeans and cotton shirts, but in their slim builds and light colouring, were setting sheet music on the stands.

136

A jet, taking off from the airport across the harbour, screamed overhead.

The storm door to Fletch's right opened.

"Mister Fletcher?"

He had not rung the bell.

Flynn's small face, at his great height, peered around the corner at him.

"Hi," Fletch said, backing away from the window he had been peering through. "How are you?"

"I'm fine," Flynn said. "Your police escort phoned me to report you were approaching my house. They fear you threaten our well-being."

"I do," said Fletch, holding out a five-pound box. "I brought your family some chocolate."

"How grand of you." Flynn held the spring door open with his huge left arm and took the candy with his right hand. "Bribery, is it?"

"It occurred to me it was the City of Boston which owed me a bottle of whisky—not the Flynn family."

Flynn said, "Come in, Fletch."

The vestibule was dark and scattered with a half-dozen pairs of rubbers. A baby carriage was parked at an odd angle.

Flynn led him into the living room.

Besides the boys in the room, one of whom now had a violin in his hands, there was a girl of about twelve with full, curly blonde hair and huge, blue saucer eyes. The colour of her short, fluffy dress matched her eyes. The boys were about fifteen.

"Munchkin," Flynn said. "This is Mister Fletcher, the murderer." Flynn pointed off his children, "Randy, Todd, Jenny."

Randy, bow and violin in one hand, extended his right. "How do you do, sir?"

As did his twin, Todd.

"Ach," said Flynn. "My family gets to meet all sorts."

A boy about nine years old entered. His hair was straight brown. Mostly he was glasses and freckles.

"This is Winny," said Flynn.

Fletch shook hands with him.

"No Francis Xavier Flynn?"

"One's enough," said Flynn. "No bloody Irwin Maurice, either."

Elizabeth Flynn entered through a door behind the piano.

Her light brown, straight hair fell to her shoulders. Her body, under her skirt and cardigan, was full and firm. Her unquestioning light blue eyes were deep-set over magnificent cheekbones. They were warm and humorous and loving.

"This is Fletch, Elsbeth. The murderer. I mentioned him."

"How do you do?" She held his hand over the music stand. "You'd like some tea, I think."

"I would."

"He brought me some candy." Flynn handed her the box. "Better give him some tea."

"How nice." She looked at the box in her hands. "Perhaps for after supper?"

"We were about to have our musicale," Flynn said. To the children, he said, "What is it today?"

"Eighteen—One." Todd's Adam's apple seemed too large for his sinewy neck, especially when he spoke. "F major."

"Beethoven? We're up to that, are we?"

Jenny said, "I am."

"Sorry to wake you all up last night," Fletch said.

Elizabeth had come in the other door with tea things.

"Come over and have a cuppa," Flynn said.

While Flynn and Fletch sat over their tea, Elizabeth at the piano helped the children tune their instruments. Todd had picked up a viola. Jenny had a less than full-sized violin.

Fletch spoke over the scrapings and plunks.

"Did you catch him?"

"Who?" Flynn poured a cup for Elizabeth as well.

"The arsonist."

"Oh, yes," said Flynn.

"Was it the gas station attendant?"

"It was a forty-three-year-old baker."

"Not the gas station attendant?"

"No."

"Oh."

"Are you crushed?"

"Why was he burning down Charlestown?"

Flynn shrugged. "Jesus told him to. Or so he said."

"But where did he get all the Astro gasoline containers?"

"He'd been saving up."

Elizabeth was tuning his 'cello.

"Now, let's see what this is all about."

Leaving his cup drained behind him, Flynn sat behind his music stand.

"Elsbeth usually joins us at the piano," he explained to Fletch, "but Beethoven didn't consider her today."

She came over to the divan and took her tea.

The children were behind their music stands.

The youngest, Winny, was the page-turner.

"Remember to turn me first," his father said. "I've got a memory like a bear's mouth."

They all straightened their backs, like flowers rising on their stems in the morning sun.

"*Con brio!*" their father shouted, in a voice of pleasant threat.

They were off, bows indicating two dimensions in their coming and going, eyes intent upon the sheet music, Randy's violin gracefully indicating, belatedly, a few notes Jenny skipped, her blue eyes getting more huge as they travelled down the page, a few times losing her place altogether (when she had nothing to play, she sighed; then her tongue would sneak out and touch the tip of her nose), Winny back and forth behind them like a waiter, following his father's score, turning his page first, then Jenny's on perfect time (frequently a help to her finding her place and a cause of renewed, more confident playing), then Todd's, then Randy's, every five or six minutes a jet screeching by just five hundred metres above the house, deafening the players (drowned out, they sawed away apparently soundlessly), making them adjust their paces to each other once they could hear each other again, ever and always Flynn's 'cello playing along, leading from behind ("*Molto! Molto!*" he shouted over the shrieking of a jet during the third section; he was enormous, delicate over his instrument), keeping the pace, somewhat, the tone, as well as it could be kept, Elizabeth sitting in the divan beside Fletch, ankles crossed, hands in her lap, loving them all with her eyes.

Upstairs, a baby mewed.

They sat rigid in their slight curve, shoulders straight, chins tucked, the boys' blue denim stretched over their slim thighs, sneakers angled on the floor like frogs' feet, the sky through the windows behind them going down the scale of grey through dusk to dark, more lights coming on at the airport across the reflecting surface of the harbour. During the fourth section, Jenny was tired and not as practised. Sighs became more frequent. The tongue crept out to the tip of her nose even when she should have been playing. Even Randy's and Todd's faces shone with perspiration.

Their hair matted on their foreheads identically. For a moment, Fletch looked at the chessmen set up on a board to his right. A game was in progress.

Jenny was vigorous in the last bars, practised, *allegro*, and, finished a little before the others. She looked momentarily confused.

It was a wonderful forty minutes.

"Bravo!" Elizabeth said while she and Fletch applauded.

"Pretty good, Jenny," Randy said, standing up.

Without comment Flynn closed his sheet music and stood to lean his 'cello in the curve of the piano again.

"Da'?" Todd said. "That should never have been in anything other than F major."

"We all make mistakes," said Flynn. "Even Beethoven. We all have our temporary madnesses."

Elizabeth was hugging Jenny and complimenting Winny on his page-turning.

It was five-twenty.

"I expect we could find a drink for you, before supper," Flynn said. "Elsbeth drinks sherry, and I suppose there's some other stuff in the house."

"I have to get to the airport," Fletch said.

"Oh?" said Flynn. "Skipping town, finally?"

Conversation was suspended while a jet thundered overhead.

The room reeked with accomplishment as the kids moved about with their instruments. They bounced on the balls of their sneakered feet as only happy, accomplished children do.

"Andy's arriving," Fletch said finally. "Six-thirty."

"Is she now? That's nice."

"You'll stay for supper?" Elizabeth said, coming back to where Fletch was now standing.

"He's picking up his girlfriend," rolled Flynn. "At the airport. That will alarm your police escort, I'm sure. I'd better warn them you don't mean to take flight, or they will tackle you at the information counter. They'll watch you, all the same."

"Bring her back with you," Elizabeth said.

Fletch shook hands respectfully with the children.

"I like you," Elizabeth said. "Frannie, this is no murderer."

"That's what all the women say," Flynn said. "I haven't convinced him yet, either."

"His face was good while he listened."

"As long as he didn't hum along," Flynn said. "Tap his toes."

They all laughed at Flynn as a jet whined in a holding pattern over their heads.

"Bring your girl back with you," shouted Elizabeth. "We'll wait supper for you!"

"Thanks anyway," said Fletch. "Really, this has been a wonderful time for me."

Flynn said, "We'd be glad to have you, Fletch."

Fletch said, "I'd be glad to stay. May I come back sometime?"

"What's your instrument?" Winny asked.

"The typewriter."

"Percussion," said Flynn.

"Well," said Elizabeth, "Leroy Anderson wrote for the typewriter."

"You come back any time," said Flynn. "Any time you're free, that is."

In the cold vestibule, Flynn said, "I guess you didn't have the conversation with me this afternoon you wanted to."

"No," said Fletch. "This was much better."

"I thought you'd think so."

"May I see you in your office tomorrow?"

"Sure."

"What's a good time?"

"Five o'clock. Any policeman with good sense is in his office at that time. The traffic is terrible."

"Okay. Where are you?"

"Ninety-nine Craigie Lane. If you get lost, ask the plainclothesmen following you."

They said good-night.

Outside, the air was damp and cold.

Fletch stood on the top step off the porch for a moment, adjusting his eyes to the dark, feeling the house's warmth at his back, hearing a bit of early Beethoven scraping in his memory's ears, thinking of the two blue doll's eyes under a doll's mop of tossed, curly blonde hair.

Across the street, under a street-light, he clearly saw the faces of the two plainclothesmen waiting for him. It seemed to him their eyes were filled with hatred.

One of them picked up the car phone as Fletch started down the steps. Flynn would be telling them Fletcher was going to the airport, and they shouldn't panic ... but to make sure he didn't get on a plane.

"Jesus Christ," Fletch said.

The scrape of his chin on his shirt collar made him realize he should have shaved.

X X X

"FLETCH!"

He had never seen Andy in an overcoat before.

After they had embraced and he had taken her hand luggage, her first question was quick and to the point.

"Is Sylvia here?"

"Yes."

"Bitch. What is she doing?"

"I don't know. I haven't seen much of her. I mean, I haven't seen her often."

"Where is she staying?"

"At my apartment."

"Where am I staying?"

"At my apartment."

"Oh, my God."

"How are you?"

Andy's big suitcase was in the way of people coming through the customs' gate. The few porters were being grabbed by artful older people.

"Any luck with the paintings?" she asked.

"Can we wait until we get in the car? How are you?"

He handed her back her purse and vanity case.

"Why did you want to know about Bart Connors?"

"How are you?"

He carried the huge suitcase through the airport, across a street, up a flight of stairs, across a bridge and halfway through the garage, to where his car was parked.

The plainsclothesmen, hands in their pockets, followed at twenty paces.

She began her questions again as he drove down the dark ramp of the airport garage.

"Where are the paintings? Do you know?"

"Not really. It's possible they're in Texas."

"Texas?"

"You and I may fly down later this week."

"How can they be in Texas?"

"Horan seems to have gotten all three de Grassi paintings from a man in Dallas named James Cooney. He's a rancher, with eight kids."

"Do you think so?"

"How do I know? I've handled Horan very carefully. His reputation is impeccable. Pompous bastard, but everything he's said so far has been straight. I'm putting a lot of pressure on him to try to crack Cooney's source."

"You mean, find out where Cooney got the paintings?"

"Yes. If putting pressure on Horan doesn't work, then we go to Texas and put pressure on Cooney ourselves."

"What did you do? You asked Horan to locate one of the paintings?"

"Yes. The bigger Picasso."

"Where is that painting now?"

"In Boston. Horan has it. I asked him for it Wednesday. He located it Thursday night or Friday morning and had it flown up Friday night. I saw it Saturday. He doubted the whole thing when I first spoke to him about it."

"What do you mean?"

"Well, he doubted whether the painting existed; whether it could be located; if it was authentic; if it was for sale."

"Is the painting authentic?"

"Yes. I'm certain as I can be. So's Horan. And, apparently, Cooney is willing to sell it."

After paying a toll, they went down a ramp into a tunnel.

Fletch spoke loudly at Andy's puzzled expression.

"So far, Horan has acted in a thoroughly professional, efficient, routine manner. I don't like him, but that's immaterial."

Driving up out of the tunnel, they faced strata of crossroads, and a vast confusion of signs and arrows.

"Oops," he said. "I don't know which way to go."

"To the right," Andy said. "Go on Storrow Drive."

"How do you know?"

He turned right from the left lane.

"We're going to Beacon Street, aren't we? Near the Gardens?"

"Yeah, but how do you know?"

They went up a ramp on to a highway.

"I lived here nearly a year," she said. "The year I was at Radcliffe."

"Where's that?"

"Cambridge. Go down there, to the right, to Storrow Drive. You knew that."

Her directions were perfect.

"Why did you want to know about Bart Connors?" she asked.

"Because the night I arrived, a girl was found murdered in his apartment."

Her profile was backed by lights reflected on the Charles River.

"He didn't do it," she said.

"You seem pretty certain."

"Yes. I am."

"That's why I yelled at you that night on the phone to get out of the villa. When I asked you to go see him, I did not expect you to take up residence with him."

"You'll want to go left here." At the red light, she craned her head left. "We'll have to go all the way around the Gardens, won't we? Dear old Boston. Or is your apartment down to the right?"

Fletch said, "The police think I did it."

"Murdered the girl? You didn't do it, either. If you did, you wouldn't be trying to blame Bart."

"Thanks."

"Bart's a very gentle man. Wouldn't hurt a fly."

"Boy, when I ask you to do a job for me.... Did you check his teeth, too?"

"His teeth," she said, "are perfectly adequate."

"My God."

"So who killed her?"

"Damn it, Andy, there's a very good chance Bart Connors did!"

"No chance whatsoever."

"He was in Boston that night when he wasn't supposed to be! He was seen two blocks away from the apartment in a pub with a girl tentatively identified as the murdered girl just before she was murdered! He had a key to his own apartment! He left on an airplane for Montreal just after the murder! And within the last six months he has received a sexual-psychological trauma, delivered by a woman, which he considered, wrongly, a blow to his masculinity!"

"I know," Andy said. "He told me all about that."

"Great."

"And he told me the night you called you were trying to lay

the crime off on him. He asked more questions about you than you've asked about him."

"Andy. . . ."

"Watch out for that taxi. Furthermore, Fletch," she continued, "I can testify that the 'sexual-psychological trauma delivered by a woman', as you phrase it, has done him no harm whatsoever."

"I bet you can."

"You and I have our understandings," she said. "Stop being stuffy."

"Stuffy? You're wearing my engagement ring."

"I know. And it's a very nice ring. Whom did you make it with this week?"

"Whom? What?"

"I didn't hear your answer. You're not acting like Fletch."

"We need a place to park."

"Over there. To the left."

"I need two places to park."

Headlights grew large in his rearview mirror.

"Absolutely," she said, "I will not help you blame Bart Connors for a crime neither of you committed."

He said, "Such loyalty."

Going up in the creaky elevator, she said, "Try Horan again."

XXXI

ON THE sixth-floor landing, Fletch put the huge suitcase down to take his keys out again, to unlock the door.

Sylvia, arms wide, in an apron, opened the door.

Andy and Sylvia clutched and jabbered simultaneously in Italian.

He had to insinuate himself, with the luggage, through the crowded front door.

They sounded like a girls' school reunion.

He understood Sylvia had prepared a magnificent supper for them. A dinner.

He left the luggage in the hall and walked empty-handed down the corridor to the telephone in the master bedroom.

145

Even through the closed door he could hear their delighted shrieks and exclamations while he dialled.

"Mister Horan? This is Peter Fletcher."

"Ah, yes, Mister Fletcher."

"Sorry to phone on a Sunday night. . . ."

"Quite all right. I'm used to calls from anywhere, at any time. Have you decided to change your offer for the Picasso?"

"Have you spoken with Mister Cooney?"

"Yes, I did. He said he won't respond to your offer at all."

"He wouldn't consider it?"

"No."

"Was he any more open regarding the painting's provenance?"

"No. I said you rightfully had questions. I outlined to him quite carefully what you had said regarding your responsibility to question the provenance. I went as far as I could, short of physically shaking him, which would be difficult over the phone, anyway."

"And you got nowhere?"

"He didn't even deign to offer the usual evasions. He said the authenticity of the painting can't really be questioned. . . ."

"Of course it can be."

"Not really. I have thoroughly satisfied myself. No, he's prepared to stand on the painting's authenticity."

"I see."

"And, by the way, Mister Fletcher, our Texas cowboy friend rather surprised me by repeating something you said."

"Oh?"

"He referred to 'Vino, Viola, Mademoiselle' as a 'most significant Picasso'. He referred to it as the 'key work of the cubist period'."

"Oh."

"So our cowboy with eight kiddies has no sheep wool over his eyes, if I may coin a phrase."

"If you insist. Mister Horan? Offer Mister Cooney five hundred and twenty-seven thousand dollars for the painting."

"Ah! Mister Fletcher. Now you're in the arena. I most certainly will."

"And you may remember originally I said I might ask you to help me on another problem or two?"

"Yes."

"I wonder if you would ask Mister Cooney if he has another particular painting in his possession?"

146

"You mean, another specific painting? I don't understand."

"Yes, another specific painting. An Umberto Boccioni entitled 'Red Space'."

" 'Red Space'? Again you've got me stumped. Mister Fletcher, you go from a key cubist work by Picasso to the work of an only relatively important Italian Futurist."

"I know."

"Fire and water."

"Or water and fire, depending upon your point of view."

"Well, again, professionally, I have to advise you that I don't know if such a painting exists. . . ."

"I do."

"What makes you think Mister Cooney might have such a painting, Mister Fletcher?"

"We all have our little secrets."

"You mean, you want me to to ask him straight out if he has this 'Red Space' by Boccioni?"

"Not necessarily 'straight out'. After all, I'm offering him over half a million dollars for the Picasso. . . ."

"It's worth much more."

"I think it's a good enough offer to justify a little conversation. You might say that someone has mentioned the existence of such a painting, and you'd give anything to be able to locate it."

"You want me to exercise craft, is that it?"

"Even deviousness," suggested Fletch. "I'll be interested in what he says."

"It's nearly eight o'clock now," Horan said. "Of course, that's not Dallas time. I guess I can try to call him tonight."

"Will you call me in the morning?"

"If I reach him."

"Thank you. Good-night."

XXXII

THE dining room table had been set with crystal and silver. The light was subdued.

"Oh, it's nothing," said Sylvia, removing her apron. "I'll serve."

Fletch sat at the far end of the table. Before leaving the room, Sylvia indicated Andy should sit to his right.

Sylvia would sit at the other end of the table.

Fletch said to Andy, "Trust you don't feel seven years old."

"What's going on here?"

"Oh!" said Fletch. "Soup!"

"The first course," said Sylvia. "A nice soup!"

In the flat bowls was about a cupful of consommé.

The bouillon cube, worn away only at its edges, sat in an island of its own grease, surrounded by cool water.

"I can tell," said Fletch. "You gave us big spoons."

Applying the tip of the spoon to the bouillon cube accomplished nothing. A minute Michelangelo with hammer and chisel might make something of it.

Stirring the water around the cube only caused it to sway like a tango dancer. The grease reached out in disgusting, finger-like patterns.

Sylvia said, "I thought we all needed a good, hot dinner! Filling and tasty! American cooking, yes?"

Fletch said, "Yes."

"After such a long airplane ride for poor, dear Angela!"

"Yes."

"This beastly, cold New England weather!"

"Yes."

"Good, hot American cooked soup!"

"Most substantial," said Fletch. "Full body, vigorous aroma, the ambience of a bus. . . ."

"You no like your soup?" Sylvia had come to collect his bowl. "You no finish your soup."

"It's taking too long to cool down."

He waved it away.

While Sylvia was in the kitchen, Andy said, "She can't cook. Everyone knows that."

"I'm finding it out."

"Now the fish!" Sylvia announced from the door. "Good American fish!"

A piece of cold, canned tuna fish and a quarter of a lemon lay on his plate.

What happened to the fourth slice of lemon?

"Oh, yeah," said Fletch. "Fish. I recognize it. Glad you removed the head, Sylvia. Never could stand a fish head on a plate. Aren't you glad she removed the head, Andy?"

"I'm glad she removed the lid."

"That, too," said Fletch. "Funny no one's ever made a solid silver can opener to go with a place setting. I'd think there'd be a market for it."

At her end of the table, Sylvia was beaming.

Her neckline disappeared into her lap. Her bilateral, upper structural support systems were more sophisticated than anything used on the Swiss railway system.

It was not the same gagging décolletage she had worn to stun the Ritz.

"Yeah." Fletch chewed the fish. "This is nice."

"Just like a family," said Sylvia.

"Precisely," said Fletch.

"Just like a family, we are together."

"Precisely like a family. Precisely."

"If only Menti were here."

"Now there was a man who knew a piece of fish when he saw one."

"Poor Menti."

"Nice touch, the slice of lemon," Fletch said. "Did you cut it yourself?"

"They've located his body," Andy said.

"Whose?"

Sylvia said, "What?"

"In a pasture. Outside Turin. The police called, just before I left."

Sylvia said, "They found Menti?"

"Really?"

"Sorry," Andy said. "I didn't mean to bring it up at dinner."

"You can't ruin dinner," Fletch said.

Sylvia began in galloping Italian exclamations (at one point, she blessed herself with her fork), ultimately giving way to long questions, which Andy answered tersely As Sylvia's questions became shorter, she switched to French—the language of reason. Andy, who had attended school in Switzerland, answered even more tersely in the language of reason.

Muttering in Portuguese, Sylvia took the fish plates into the kitchen.

"Now it's my turn," said Fletch.

"The police called just before I left. They found the body in a shallow grave in a pasture outside Turin."

"Do they know it's your father?"

"His age, his height, his weight. They're pretty sure. Dead about three weeks."

"I see."

Sylvia entered with salad plates. The salad consisted of a clump of cold, canned peas huddled together against the rim. On none of the plates had any of the peas broken free of the clump.

"Oh," said Fletch, "a pea."

"Salad!" Sylvia screwed herself into her chair. "Good American salad!"

She had added salt. Too much salt.

"I would think," Fletch spoke quietly, "if that were the case, one of you, if not both, should be in Italy to receive the remains."

" 'Remains?' " asked Sylvia. "What's 'remains'?"

Fletch said, "Sort of like supper."

Andy answered her properly in Italian.

Quickly, Sylvia said, "This is not to be spoken of at dinner."

"I thought not," said Fletch.

"Angela," the Countess demanded archly, "why you no stay to accept your father's remains?"

"The police want them."

"Why the police want the remains of Menti?"

Sylvia was getting a remarkable amount of chewing out of her pea.

"They said they had much to do."

"What to do? What to do with the remains of Menti?"

"They have to test his teeth."

"What's wrong with Menti's teeth? He's dead! No good testing them now!"

Fletch said, "That's how they confirm the identification of a corpse, Sylvia. The body's been in the ground three weeks."

"Oh. If the body is wearing Menti's teeth, then they know it is Menti?"

"Yes."

"Ha!" said Sylvia, for some reason victoriously, fork in air. "Menti had no teeth!"

"What?"

"All Menti's teeth false! His gums were entirely—how you say?—bareass."

"That's right," said Andy. "I had forgotten that."

"They can identify a corpse by its false teeth," Fletch said.

"How come you know so much?" Sylvia asked.

Andy said, "The police said they would give us a closed coffin when they are through doing what they can to identify father. We can have a burial. It doesn't matter when. We've already had the funeral."

"This is terrible," said Sylvia. "Poor Menti."

Something was sizzling in the kitchen, suggesting the threat of a fourth course.

"Did you have a chance to speak to the lawyers?" Fletch asked Andy.

"Yes. I called Mister Rosselli. He said it was good news."

"That your father was murdered?"

"We knew he was murdered. The police said so."

"Sorry."

"He said the will could be read after he gets the papers from the police."

"What papers?" exploded Sylvia. "Already we have had papers up the asses!"

"They have to have positive identification, Sylvia," Fletch said. "They can't settle an estate without a corpse."

"Pash!" She shook her fork in the air. "All they want is Menti's teeth! You look in that closed coffin. There will be no teeth! Some police inspector in Turin will wear them!"

Fletch said, "Sylvia. Something is burning."

"Ooo," she said, grabbing up her gown for the run to the kitchen.

In their momentary privacy, Fletch said to Andy: "I guess I'm tired."

She said, "That's why we're having such a nice dinner."

"I should have planned something."

"Yes. You should have."

"I never guessed Sylvia would make such an effort."

Andy said, "I don't guess she has."

The entrée was a burned frankfurter each, sliced lengthwise. At the edge of each plate was a tomato, obviously hand-squeezed. The indentations of four fingers and a thumb were clear. In fact, Sylvia's thumb-print was clear.

"Oh, my God," Fletch said.

"What's the matter?" Sylvia was screwing herself into her chair again. "Good American meal! Hot dog! Ketchup!"

Andy said, "Sylvia, really!"

"You live in America, you get used to American food," Sylvia said. "I been here nearly one week already. See?"

"We see," said Fletch.

"Bastard Rosselli say what Menti's will say about my paintings?"

Fletch said, "What paintings? There are no paintings."

"There are paintings." In her insistence, Sylvia leaned so far forward she almost dipped one in the 'catsup'. "My paintings you two find. If you no look for, why you here? If you no find, why Angela come? Eh? Answer me that, Mister Flesh Ass-pants."

Fletch said, "We just came for dinner."

"Rosselli said nothing about the will, Sylvia."

Fletch said, "I'm in love with Jennifer Flynn."

He made no approach to his frankfurter and tomato. They sat there, burned and thumbprinted, like a victim and a perpetrator.

Andy, using her knife and fork on the frankfurter, was looking at him.

He said, "I would think you'd both want to be in Rome now."

"No!" said Sylvia. "I stay here. Where my paintings are."

Looking at Sylvia, Fletch counted the number of hours of sleep he had had. Then he counted the number of hours of sleep he hadn't had.

"Sylvia," he said. "The paintings are in Texas."

"Texas?"

"Andy and I are planning to fly to Dallas the end of this week."

"Good! Then I go, too."

"Good!" said Fletch. "We'll all go. Just like a family."

Andy's look could have burned through telephone books.

To Andy he said, "I doubt you've ever had Texan chili. Good American cooking."

"Chili sauce," said Sylvia. "You want chili sauce?"

Fletch placed his unused napkin next to his untouched plate.

"Sorry I can't stay to help out with the dishes. I'm going to sleep now."

"Sleep?" Sylvia was prepared to be hurt. "You no want dessert?"

"Don't even tell me what it is," Fletch said. "I'll dream on it."

He went into a guest room, locked the door, stripped, and crawled between the sheets.

The rhythms of exclamations in Italian, French, Portuguese and English through the thick walls lulled him to hungry sleep.

XXXIII

"HI, BABE."

In the single bed, he had rolled on to his side.

Light was pouring through the open drapes.

Eyes open, staring at him, her head faced him on the pillow.

The white sheet over her upper arm perfected her smooth, tanned shoulder, neck, throat.

His right hand went along her left breast, under her arm, down her side. She pulled her right leg up, to touch his.

"Nice to feel you again," he said.

She must have entered through the bathroom from the other guest room.

He flicked her lips with his tongue.

Then his left arm went under her and found the small of her back and brought her closer to him.

"Where were you last night?" she asked.

"When?"

"Two o'clock. Three o'clock. You weren't in bed."

"I went out for a walk," he said. "After that heavy dinner."

In fact, between two and three in the morning, he had switched the licence plates of the rented car and the black truck.

" 'After that heavy dinner'," she said.

She giggled.

"Did you use my bed in Cagna?" he asked.

"Of course. Our bed."

He said, "I'm hungry."

She put on a slightly perplexed face.

She said, "This is your apartment."

"Yes."

"How come Sylvia's in the master bedroom and you and I are in a single bed in a guest room?"

"I don't know."

"You don't know?"

"I guess it's like the Latin-American expression, 'I lost the battle of the street'."

"Was there a revolution?"

"There must have been. I guess I was an absentee government."

"What does that mean?"

"I wasn't here a couple of nights."

"Where were you?"

"I was working."

"Working?"

"At a newspaper. An old boy I worked with in Chicago works for a paper here now. He was shorthanded and asked me to come in. Charlestown was burning down again."

"Why would you do that?"

"Why not?"

"Why should you?"

"I liked it. Anyhow, Jack had let me spend some time at the newspaper looking up Horan."

"Jack?"

"Jack Saunders."

"I doubt it would take two nights for Charlestown to burn down."

"What do you mean?"

"I mean, I would expect your friend to solve his staff problems by the second night."

"I don't get you."

"You said you were gone two nights."

"Did I say that?"

"Where were you the other night?"

"What other night?"

"You were only gone one night?"

"Ah...."

"If you were only gone one night, how come Sylvia has the master bedroom?"

"Um...."

"How come she has it, anyway."

"Who? Sylvia?"

"Were you sleeping with Sylvia?"

"Who, me?"

"You see, Fletch?"

"See what?"

"Don't give me a hard time."

"Did I give you a hard time?"

"About Bart."

"Oh, yeah, Bart the Woman Slayer."

"He needed help, Fletch."

"I'll bet."

"You know why his wife left him?"

"I heard rumours."

"Then this girl he wanted to take to Cagna finally refused to go."

"I know. I found her body. She should have gone."

"Bart never killed anybody."

"Andy, one of three people killed Ruth Fryer. I know I didn't, and Bart tops the list of the other two candidates."

"Tell me about Sylvia."

"Sylvia who?"

"Come on."

"You must have misunderstood something."

"I did not. You're never lost a battle of the street in your life."

"I haven't known many Sylvias."

"What happened?"

"I was raped."

"That's nice."

"Not bad."

"I don't believe you."

"Believe me. I think you've figured out she wants the paintings as much as you do."

"She's not going to get them, is she?"

"I know what she has to offer. What do you have to offer?"

"You know what I have to offer."

"You're skinnier than she is."

"You like that. Skinny."

"Did I say that?"

"Once or twice."

"Was I telling the truth?"

"One never knows."

"We're doing an awful lot of talking. For two friends who haven't seen each other in almost a week."

"I'm not used to making deals in bed."

"Oh. Then feel sorry for me."

"Why should I feel sorry for you?"

"I was raped. I need to get my sexual confidence back."

"You have it back. I can feel it."

"See how much good you've done already?"

XXXIV

F L E T C H went into the den to answer the telephone after a second helping of scrambled eggs and sausage.

It was past ten, and Sylvia apparently had gone out earlier to follow her own investigation, which, Fletch guessed, meant walking through Boston's private galleries with the list of de Grassi paintings in her hand.

It was, finally, a cloudless October day.

At breakfast, Fletch and Andy had decided to spend the day walking the old streets. She said she would show him his American history.

He worried about the moon.

It was Horan.

"Mister Fletcher, I was able to get Mister Cooney on the phone last night, too late to call you back."

"That was very considerate of you. I did go to bed early."

"There was little point in rushing to you with the news anyway."

"Oh?"

"He says he won't respond to your new offer for the Picasso, either. Contrary to my advice to you, he says you're not even in the ballpark."

"Did you remind him he has eight kids to feed?"

"He said he is looking for upwards of a million dollars for the painting."

"Hungry kids. I thought beef was cheaper in Texas."

"That's the lay of the land. I don't know if you want to go further with this negotiation, but I expect you'll want to think about it."

"Would you? I mean, would you go further?"

"I think I would. I think I'd make another offer for it. Of course, I have no idea how much of your resources you want to tie up in a single property."

"Will you make another offer, if I don't?"

"Mister Fletcher, I think I made a mistake there—one for which I apologize—in indicating to you I might be interested in purchasing this painting if you don't. I'm your broker, in this case, and a client should never feel he would be in a position where he must bid against his own broker."

"I was wondering about that."

"I was greatly mistaken. What I meant was, if this negotiation between you and Cooney doesn't work out, after a decent interval of time—and it would be a long, decent interval—I might reopen negotiations with Mister Cooney on my own, or even, conceivably, on behalf of another client."

"I see."

"As long as you leave your negotiation with Mister Cooney open, you will not be bidding against me, or any other client of mine, even potentially. I will continue to give you my best advice, to make your negotiation successful."

"And what's your advice now?"

"First, I think you should think about it. No reason for being too swift in these matters. After you consider your own resources, and the very real question of how much of those resources you want committed to a single property, I'd make a new offer, if I were so inclined."

"How much?"

"The new offer? I think eight hundred thousand dollars."

"I'll think about it."

"All right, Mister Fletcher. Call me any time."

"What about the other painting?"

"What other painting?"

"The Boccioni. 'Red Space'."

"Oh. A complete blank."

"Really?"

"I guess I was too subtle at first. He had no idea what I was talking about. I finally asked him, more directly. Mister Cooney clearly had never heard of Umberto Boccioni."

"That's puzzling."

"I guess your source of information was dead wrong."

"That's hard to believe."

"Nothing's hard to believe in this business, Mister Fletcher. Whoever told you Mister Cooney owns a Boccioni was incorrect. Call me when you decide about the Picasso."

"I will."

Andy was clearing the dishes from the dining room table.

"That was Horan," Fletch said. "Our man in Texas never heard of Umberto Boccioni."

XXXV

Trusting the two plainclothesmen would not be too puzzled by his not using the Ford Ghia, Fletch took a taxi to Flynn's office on Craigie Lane.

It was a greystone pile at the edge of Boston Harbour. Inside, everything was painted regulation green, except the sagging wood floors, which were soft underfoot.

The policeman behind the counter sent him up a curved staircase with a heavy, carved wooden railing.

Grover was making tea in a corridor alcove on the second floor. He led Fletch into Flynn's office.

Flynn was behind an old, wooden desk, and behind him three arched, almost cathedral-like windows overlooked the harbour. A few straight-backed, wooden chairs stood about the room in no particular order. Along the inside wall was a long, wooden refectory table.

"Did you bring Mister Fletcher a cup of tea as well, Grover?" Flynn stood up to shake hands. "Pull up a pew, Mister Fletcher. Make yourself at home."

Grover placed the two tea cups at the edge of the desk and went out to get a third.

"We'll have a nice little tea party."

Fletch moved one of the wooden chairs to be at an angle to the desk so he would have solid wall behind Flynn, not the late afternoon light from the windows.

"Homey," said Fletch.

"I know." Behind his desk, Flynn's elfin face looked like that of a schoolboy playing teacher. "I came to look at you in an off-moment, Saturday, and you came to look at me in an off-moment, Sunday. That was our weekend. I learned you're a peeping tom, besides being a reporter and a murderer, either one of which is bad enough, but did we accomplish anything else?"

After handing Fletch a cup of tea, without questions regarding cream and sugar (there was neither in the cup), Grover took his own cup, and dragged a chair over to the long table against the wall.

"You do want me to take notes, Inspector?"

"For what they're worth. I think Mister Fletcher has something important to say, and I want a witness."

Fletch asked, "How's the other murder going? The chubby City Councilperson's murder?"

"Slowly," said Reluctant Flynn. "Very time-consuming, to be sure."

"Was the axe murder solved?"

"Oh, of course. Such things are usually family matters. I don't know why we bother with them at all."

"Look, regarding the Ruth Fryer business. . . ."

"It's called murder."

"Yes. I want off the hook."

"You want to go to Texas."

"Probably."

"We'll be pleased to let you off the hook as soon as we find a more attractive candidate for charging than yourself."

Fletch said, "I would guess not too much has been accomplished in recent days."

"Will you listen to that, Grover? The candidate for hanging is getting impatient. And he had such a great lot of faith in the institution of the Boston Police to begin with."

At the side of the room, Grover sat hunched over his table, writing slowly.

"I quite understand you've got other things to do," Fletch said.

"One or two. One or two."

"And undoubtedly there's a lot of political and press pressure on you regarding the City Councilperson's murder."

"I thank you for making my excuses."

"But I'm being sort of a victim here. I didn't kill Ruth Fryer."

"You say you didn't."

"And the investigation has been dragging on almost a week now."

"Mister Fletcher, the Complaint Department is downstairs. It's a small room, with see-through walls."

"Another person in my position might have hired private detectives this last week. . . ."

"However, being a great ex-investigative reporter yourself, you've done a little investigating on your own. Is that it?"

"Yes."

"And have you come to a conclusion?"

"I think I have."

"Do you want time to sharpen your pencil, Grover? Oh, it's a pen. I don't want you to miss a word."

"Okay," said Fletch. "First of all, it is most likely the murderer must have had a key to the apartment. Not absolutely necessary. Thinking Bart Connors was in Italy and the apartment was empty, Ruth Fryer could have gone to the apartment alone or with some other person to use the apartment for sexual purposes. Or, not knowing Connors was in Italy, to surprise him. She could have had a key, which the murderer then took. Or Joan Winslow, in a state of advanced intoxication, could have let her in."

"All highly unlikely," said Flynn. "The Winslow woman supposedly was at the Bullfinch Pub. Ruth Fryer would have seen your suitcases in the hall, noted the airline's tags in the name of Peter Fletcher and been scared off from whichever course of action she intended. For the last time, Mister Fletcher, I reject the idea that Ruth Fryer killed herself."

"Narrow of you," said Fletch, "but I accept it. So," he continued, "the basic question is, who had a key to that apartment? Me," he counted himself off on his little finger, "Mrs. Sawyer, whom you've investigated...."

"As pure as Little Eva."

"... Joan Winslow...."

"Ach, she's incapable of anything."

"... Bart Connors...."

"Now he's a real possibility. How come we haven't thought of him, Grover?"

"... and Lucy Connors."

"Lucy Connors?"

"Let's consider Bart Connors first."

"You've been considering Bart Connors from the very beginning. You've been after him so, the man has my sympathy."

"Apparently." Fletch was hanging on to his index finger. "Six months ago, Bart Connors had a sexual-psychological shock. His wife left him, for a woman. Mrs. Sawyer said he then became sexually very active. He is known to have brought girls to his apartment. We thought he had gone to Italy on Sunday. He did not leave Boston until nine-thirty Tuesday night, and then he flew through Montreal, a sort of unusual thing to do. Just prior to the murder, Joan Winslow said she saw him in a pub two blocks away with a girl she has identified as Ruth Fryer."

"She's an unreliable witness. Any defence attorney would make hash of her in minutes."

"Flynn, why isn't Bart Connors the murderer?"

"I don't know."

"We know he delayed his departure from Boston because he was trying to talk a girl into going to Italy with him—a girl who ultimately refused."

"Well, I have a prejudice against him. He's a Boston lawyer, you know, an important firm. . . ."

"All of which just means he's smart enough to lay the crime off on someone else."

"I don't know why he'd need to. I don't know why he wouldn't have taken the body and dumped it in some alley."

"He had a plane to catch. He was well-known in the neighbourhood. It was still early evening. He knew I'd be arriving."

"All good reasons. But Ruth Fryer had not had sexual intercourse."

"That's it, Flynn. Her rejecting him, after his experience with his wife, may have sent him up the wall."

"May have."

"Frankly, Flynn, I don't think you've paid enough attention to Bart Connors as a suspect."

"Grover, pay more attention to Bart Connors as a suspect."

"Incidentally, something else you don't know is that Ruth Fryer's boyfriend, whose name is Clay Robinson, flew up from Washington Tuesday afternoon to spend a few days with her."

"Did he? Grover, our incompetence is becoming marked."

"Presuming Ruth Fryer knew Bart Connors, and thought he was in Italy, why wouldn't she have taken Clay Robinson to use Bart's apartment?"

"Why would she, when there are hotels?"

"It's a nice place."

"Wouldn't she have had to explain to her boyfriend how it was she had access to such an apartment?"

"I suppose so."

"She had no key we know of, Mister Fletcher. Your tagged luggage was in the hall. . . ."

"Okay. Now we come to Joan Winslow."

"My God, Grover, it's like listening to one of those Harvard-Radcliffe professors—such a pompous lecture we're getting."

"Flynn, I'm tired of being a murder suspect."

"I'd say you've got pretty good evidence those paintings are in Texas." Flynn's voice was barely audible across the desk. "You want to get out of here."

"Inspector, I didn't catch that," Grover said.

"You weren't meant to. Go on, Mister Fletcher."

"Joan Winslow has a key to the apartment. She was in love with Bart Connors. Passionately. He had rejected her quite thoroughly. She hated, absolutely hated, the young girls he had been bringing to his apartment."

"So how would that work in time and space?"

"I don't know. Joan Winslow heard someone in Bart's apartment, knew he was in Italy, went over to investigate, found Ruth Fryer naked, thinking she was waiting for Bart; Joan went into a drunken rage and slugged her with the bottle."

"Who put the other whisky bottles away? I mean, cleaned off the whole liquor bar?"

"Joan Winslow did. She knew the apartment. I guess she knew I was coming in. Or, she saw the suitcases and knew I was going to return. Or, she simply wanted to frame Bart Connors."

"That's a possibility."

"Joan Winslow has made an even greater effort than I have to blame Bart Connors. She identified Ruth Fryer as being the girl she saw in the pub with him."

"When do we get to consider all the evidence against you? Grover's getting anxious over there."

"I think you've done enough of that. You've considered me such a prime suspect, you've done little else."

"Now, what haven't we done?"

"I'll tell you what you haven't done. You didn't find Ruth Fryer's motel key."

"By the way, you never gave it to me."

"You didn't need it. You didn't know Joan Winslow has a key to Bart Connors' apartment."

"That was thick of us. Sheer inexperience on my part."

"You didn't know Ruth Fryer's boyfriend, Clay Robinson, was in Boston Tuesday afternoon."

"How were we to know that?"

"You haven't talked with Bart Connors."

"Oh. Him again. You sound like a Christmas phonograph—reindeer and snowflakes and bright shining stars over and over again."

"And the most significant thing of all I don't even think you've thought of doing."

"We've had the City Councilperson's murder. . . ."

"You're not going to send me to prison, Flynn, because you're distracted."

"Such a scolding I'm getting. You sound like Grover. A more experienced policeman might resent it."

"Sorry, Flynn, but I want to get moving."

"You've mentioned it."

"Lucy Connors," said Fletch.

"Ah, yes. Lucy Connors."

"She has a key to the apartment."

"Has she? Have you talked with her?"

"Yes."

"Very enterprising of you. When could that have been? Does she live in Brookline?"

"Yes."

"Ah. You went there Sunday morning, before paying your visit to me."

"Flynn, Lucy Connors flew into Boston from Chicago Tuesday afternoon on Trans World Airlines."

"My God."

"Furthermore, she made an excuse to her room-mate for being late. She was late by two or three hours."

"Very enterprising of you, Mister Fletcher. Very enterprising, indeed."

"She has a history of violence, which she admits. She used to beat up her husband—send him to the office with welts. She and her girlfriend still play with sexual violence."

"You must have been a very good investigative reporter, Mister Fletcher, to know what two people do in bed."

"Lucy Connors flies into Boston. Her eye is taken by Ground Hostess Ruth Fryer. She picks her up, maybe with some story about her boutique. Ruth is young and innocent, and never dreams this older woman has sexual designs on her. They go to Ruth's hotel, where she changes into a pretty dress, because, after all, this older woman, her new friend, has been in Chicago buying for her boutique. She doesn't wait for Clay Robinson, because she doesn't know he's coming. Ruth is an airline stewardess, bored in a city she doesn't know, about to get married in a month or two; another girl asks her to join her for drinks, a dinner, the evening. Why shouldn't she go? She feels perfectly safe."

"We have to think in these terms, don't we?" said Flynn.

"A man and a woman can check into a hotel together, but eyebrows still rise at two women doing so."

"I expect so."

"Lucy can't take Ruth Fryer home with her, because Marsha is at the apartment, waiting."

"So," said Flynn, "knowing Bart's in Italy—either not knowing about your arrival, or not caring as she has a perfect right to use the Connors apartment, they not being divorced yet—she brings Ruth Fryer to what is technically your apartment at that point."

"Yeah. And at the apartment, Ruth discovers she, in fact, is being seduced. She's a young girl, she's about to be married, she's not that way. She's straight. She resists. Her dress gets torn from her. She runs down the hall. Lucy, who enjoys violent play, chases her down the hall. Also, Lucy is not very experienced at seducing girls. She loses her head. Maybe she's hurt at being rejected. Maybe she goes into a blind rage."

"And she cracks little Ms. Fryer over the head with a whisky bottle."

"Dusts the bottle and puts it back. She puts all the other bottles in the salt-and-pepper cabinet, knowing Mrs. Sawyer will have to move them around. Her own fingerprints wouldn't make any difference, anyway."

"And she puts out a carafe of water, knowing that when you return to the apartment and find the body after dinner, it would be any man's normal instinct to pour himself a stiff one at the sideboard. Thus she got your fingerprints on the murder weapon."

"Right."

"Damned clever. How did you get to interview Lucy Connors?"

"I said I was from a magazine."

"I see. It seems you've done better than we have, Fletcher."

"The thing that has been puzzling since the beginning," said Fletch, "is that this murder appeared to be a crime of sexual passion. The victim was naked. She was beautiful. And yet the autopsy turned up no evidence of sexual intercourse."

"That was surprising," said Flynn.

"There would be no such evidence, if the sexual affair was lesbian."

"My God, it's been in front of our eyes all the time."

"Lucy has a key. She and Ruth were at the airport at the same time. She would be attracted to Ruth. Anyone would be. She and Ruth could not go to a hotel, easily or safely. Lucy is known to be violence-prone. Ruth would have resisted her."

"An arrest," said Flynn, standing up from his desk, "is imminent."

"58 Fenton Street, Brookline," said Fletch, also standing. "Apartment 42. Under the name of Marsha Hauptmann."

"Have you got that, Grover?"

164

"Yes, Inspector."

"Now, Frank," said Fletch. "Would you do me a favour?"

"It seems I owe you one."

"Get your goons off my back."

"I will, indeed. Grover, order Mister Fletcher's tail removed immediately."

"Yes, sir."

"And will you be at home later tonight, Mister Fletcher?"

"I expect to be. Later."

"Perhaps I'll give you a call to tell you how things turn out."

"I'd appreciate that."

"I'm sure you will, Mister Fletcher. I'm sure you will."

XXXVI

BOTH Andy and Sylvia marvelled when Fletch donned blue jeans, boots, a dark blue turtle neck sweater, Navy windbreaker, and a Greek fisherman's cap, and said he was going out for a while.

He said he would be back for dinner.

He wouldn't.

Although free of his police tail, out of habit he went through the kitchen and down the service stairs of the apartment house. Going through the alley to his garage on River Street was a short cut, anyway.

In the black truck, Fletch put himself on Newbury Street and headed west. (The two top storeys of 60 Newbury Street were lit.) He crossed Massachusetts Avenue, down the ramp, and continued west on the Massachusetts Turnpike Extension.

Lolling along, singing to himself while munching pretzels, he took the Weston exit, went left at a light, and curved right up a grade after a second light. The moon was out. Climbing, after he passed the golf course, he had a better view of the antique farmhouses, close to the road, and the well-separated estate houses, set back.

Passing the Horan house, he noted it showed no light.

He continued on into Weston Centre.

Next to a drugstore on the main road was a lit telephone booth. Fletch parked at an angle, next to it, and checked his watch.

It was five minutes past nine Monday night. He had been in Massachusetts about six days and six hours.

Despite the dim light emanating from the drugstore, he knew it was closed.

In the phone booth, he dialled the Boston number of Ronald Risom Horan.

The man answered immediately.

Chewing gum in mouth, thumb pressed against his left nostril, Fletch said, "Mister Horan? Yeah. This is the Weston police. Your burglar alarm just went off. Yeah. The light just lit on the console here."

"Is someone at the house now?"

"Yeah! A burglar is, I guess."

"Are the police there?"

"Oh, yeah. We're sending the car over. As soon as we can locate it."

"What do you mean, as soon as you locate it?"

"Yeah, they're not answering the radio just now."

"Jesus! Listen, you jerk! Get someone to the house right away!"

"Yeah. I'll do what I can."

"I'll be out right away."

"Yeah. Okay. You know where the police station is?"

"I'm not going to the police station, you jerk! I'm going to the house!"

The phone slammed down.

Taking his time, Fletch drove back to Horan's house, down the driveway.

He drove behind the house to the garage. His headlights picked up the dirt track around the right of the garage. He drove around the garage. His headlights swept the area as he turned.

He backed the black truck into the tractor shed and turned out the headlights.

Walking back around the garage, he saw that the back and side of the house were bathed in moonlight. It was easy to find a big enough stone.

On the back porch, being careful to lay his bare fingers nowhere but on the stone, he re-examined the alarm system carefully. There were six small panes of glass in the back door. Each

166

pane had two wires of the alarm system zigzagging through it, from left to right, top and bottom.

Very carefully, with the stone, he smashed the pane of glass nearest the door handle, knocking out both wires.

The alarm went off—a high, excited, shrill, piercing, truly frightening ringing.

His mind's eye saw a light beginning to flash at a console at the Weston police station.

As he went down the porch stairs, he pitched the stone into the woods.

He crossed the driveway to the bushes. In the bright moonlight, he stood, silently, further back in the bushes than he wanted to, but he still had clear views of the driveway, the side and back of the house.

Soon he saw the huge lights of the Rolls-Royce travelling north on the road. It braked as it approached the driveway.

The lights streamed down the gravel.

Horan turned the car so the headlights flooded the back porch of the house. He dashed across the gravel and up the steps. His feet crunched on the broken glass. He stooped to examine the window. Using his key, he let himself into the house.

The kitchen light went on.

In a moment, the burglar alarm was turned off.

No lights went on in the front of the house.

Dim lights, as from a stairwell, mixed with the moonlight on the window surfaces at the back of the house, both downstairs and upstairs.

Then lights went on in an upstairs room at the back of the house. Light poured through its two windows.

Other than the kitchen, the room in the centre of the second storey was the only room fully lit.

There was a noise from the road to Fletch's left.

Blue lights rotating on the top of a police car came down the driveway. There was no sound of a siren.

The policemen parked behind the Rolls. Going around it, one of the policemen brushed his fingers along a fender.

Horan appeared at the back door.

"You Mister Horan?"

"What took you guys so goddamned long?"

"We came as soon as we got the call."

"Like hell you did. I got out from Boston sooner."

"Is this your car?"

"Never mind about that. What the hell am I paying taxes for, if this is the kind of protection I get?"

The policemen were climbing the steps, their wide belts and holsters making them look heavy-hipped.

"You pay your taxes, Mister Horan, because you have to."

"What's your name?"

"Officer Cabot, sir. Badge number 92."

The other policeman said, "The glass is smashed, Chuck."

"Christ," said Horan.

"Anything missing?" asked Cabot.

"No."

"The alarm must have scared them off."

"The alarm had to scare them off," said Horan. "Nothing else would."

"We can patch that up with a piece of plywood and some tacks."

Cabot said, "Let's look around, anyway."

Lights went on and off throughout the whole house as Horan showed them around.

The ground was cold. Fletch began to feel it in his boots.

The three men were fiddling about the back door. The policemen were helping Horan tack a piece of plywood on the inside of the door, over the window frames.

"You live here, or in Boston?"

"Both places."

"You should get this window fixed first thing in the morning."

"You're no one to tell me my business," said Horan.

The policemen came down the steps and ambled towards their car.

From the porch, Horan said, "Get here a little faster next time, will you?"

Turning, the car reversed and headed up the driveway. Its rotating blue lights went out.

Horan returned to the house and turned out all the lights.

He closed and locked the back door.

Moving slowly, he came down the porch steps, got into the car, reversed it a few metres, and drove up the driveway.

As soon as the Rolls' tail-lights disappeared around the curve, Fletch hurried across the driveway and up the porch steps.

Using his handkerchief over his hand, he pressed in on the plywood through the broken window. The tacks pushed free easily. The wood clattered on to the kitchen floor.

Stooping a little, at an angle, he reached his arm through the window as far as his elbow. He released the locks and opened the door from inside.

Quickly, he snapped on the kitchen light.

Anyone roused by the alarm and still watching the house would think they were seeing a continuation of the previous action, Fletch hoped. The house had been completely dark for only a minute or two.

Turning on lights as he went, he ran up the back stairs, along a short corridor, and into the centre back room. The light revealed what was obviously an antiseptic, unlived-in guest bedroom with a huge closet.

The closet door was unlocked.

Light from the bedroom caused shadows from what appeared to be three white, bulky objects—each leaning against a wall of the closet.

He pulled a chain hanging from a bare light bulb in the centre of the closet.

In the centre of the closet, on the floor, was a Degas horse.

He lifted it into the bedroom.

Gently, he tugged the dust sheets away from the paintings stacked neatly, resting against each other's frames, against the closet walls.

He lifted two paintings out of the closet.

One was the smaller Picasso.

The other was a Modigliani.

These were the de Grassi collection. Sixteen objects, including the horse.

He took the Picasso and the Modigliani downstairs with him and left them in the kitchen.

Then he ran to the tractor shed for the truck.

He backed it against the back porch and opened its back doors.

He put the two paintings from the kitchen into it, bracing them carefully, face down, on the tarpaulin.

It took him half an hour to load the truck.

Before he left the house, he closed the closet door and wiped his fingerprints off its handle. As he went through the house, he turned off all the lights, giving the switches a wipe with his handkerchief as he did so.

In the kitchen, he replaced the plywood against the broken window, fitting the tacks into their original holes and pressing them firm.

Driving along the highway, back into Boston, he maintained the speed limit precisely.

Fletch continued to have a professionally jaundiced view of the police, but, under the circumstances, there was no sense in taking chances.

XXXVII

"MISTER Fletcher? This is Francis Flynn."

"Yes, Inspector."

"Did I wake you up?"

It was quarter to twelve, midnight.

"Just taking a shower, Inspector."

"I am in the process of exercising two warrants. Is that how a real policeman would say it?"

"I don't know."

"In any case, I am."

"Good."

"The first is for the arrest of Ronald Risom Horan for the murder of Ruth Fryer."

Fletch kept listening, but Flynn said no more.

"What?"

"Horan killed Ruth Fryer. Would you believe that, now?"

"No."

"It's as true as the devil inhabits fleas."

"It's not possible. Horan?"

"Himself. He's in the back of a car now on his way to be booked at headquarters. Sure, and there's no knowing what's in a man's heart. A respectable man like that." Fletch listened, breathing through his mouth. "We had to wait for the man to get home. He says he took a ride in the country by himself, on this beautiful moonlit night. And, of course, we had to use a pretext to get to see him at all, such an exclusive dealer in art he is, sitting here by himself in this castle. I borrowed a page from your book, if you don't mind—the book you haven't written yet— and made an appointment with him by saying I had a small Ford Madox Brown I had to sell. Do I have that name right?"

"Yes."

"And I said it was a nineteenth-century English work, to show him I knew my potatoes. Was that right?"

"Yes, Inspector."

"Anyway, it must have worked, because he made the appointment with me. Serving the warrant was the easy matter. I let Grover do it. The lad gets such satisfaction from telling people they're under arrest, especially for murder."

"Inspector, something's...."

"The second warrant is to search both this house and the house in Weston for the de Grassi paintings."

"Weston? What house in Weston?"

"Horan has a house in Weston. That's a little town about twelve miles to the west of us. So Grover says."

"There's no Weston address listed for him in *Who's Who*."

"I think your Mister Horan keeps his cards pretty close to his necktie, if you know what I mean. He's not in the telephone book out there, either."

"Then why do you think he has a house in Weston?"

"We have our resources, Mister Fletcher."

"Inspector, something's...."

"Now what I'm asking is this: seeing you're such a distinguished writer-on-the-arts, and all, and therefore can be counted on to recognize the de Grassi paintings, I wonder if you'd be good enough to join me in my treasure hunt? I'm at the Horan Gallery now."

"You are?"

"I am. We'll have a look around here, and if we find nothing, we'll go out to Weston together and have a look around that house."

"We will?"

"You don't mind, do you?"

"Inspector, what makes you think Horan has the paintings? He's a dealer. He works on assignments for other people."

"I've sent Grover to your address. He'll be sitting outside your door in a matter of minutes, if he's not there already. If you'd pull up your braces, however late in the night it is, and let him drive you over here, I'd be deeply in your debt."

"Inspector, something's...."

"I know, Mister Fletcher. Something's wrong. Will you come and correct the error in my ways?"

"Of course, Inspector."

"There's a good lad."

Fletch left his hand on the receiver a moment after hanging up. It was sweating.

In the guest bedroom, he threw his jeans and sweater in the back of a bureau drawer and began to dress quickly in a tweed suit.

From the bed, Andy said, "Who was that?"

"The police. Flynn."

"Where are you going?"

"He's arrested Horan for the murder of Ruth Fryer."

She sat up in bed.

"The girl?"

"He's flipped his lid."

Sylvia, in a flowing nightdress, was in the corridor.

Fletch got just a flash of her fenders as he dashed by.

"What happens? Where you go now? Angela! What happens?"

Fletch ran down the five flights to the lobby.

A black four-door Ford was double-parked in front of the apartment building.

Fletch glanced down the street, at where the black truck was parked in front of the Ford Ghia.

He got into the front passenger seat.

Grover turned the ignition key.

Fletch said, "Hi, Grover."

Grover put the car in gear and started down Beacon Street.

"My name's not Grover," he said.

"No?"

"No. It's Whelan. Richard T. Whelan."

"Oh."

He said, "Sergeant Richard T. Whelan."

Going around the corner into Newbury Street, Fletch said, "Quite a man, your boss."

Sergeant Richard T. Whelan said, "He's a bird's turd."

XXXVIII

T H E street door of the Horan Gallery was open.

Fletch closed it, aware what an open door would do to the building's climate control, and ran up the stairs to Horan's office.

Flynn was sitting behind Horan's Louis Seize desk, going through the drawers.

The Picasso, "Vino, Viola, Mademoiselle", was still on the easel.

"Ah, there he is now," said Flynn. "Peter Fletcher."

"This is one of the paintings," said Fletch.

"I thought it might be. Lovely desk this, too. Pity I haven't a touch of larceny in me."

Fletch stood between the painting and the desk, hands in his jacket pockets.

"Inspector, just because Horan has this painting does not mean that he has the other de Grassi paintings."

"I think it does." Reluctantly, Flynn stood up from behind the desk. "Come. We'll take a quick tour around the house. You'll recognize anything else that belongs to the de Grassis?"

"Yes."

"Good. Then all we need do is walk around."

"Inspector, this painting, this Picasso, is here because I asked Horan to locate it and negotiate my purchase of it. A man named Cooney sent it up from Texas."

"I see."

On the landing, Flynn was stepping into a small elevator.

"In talking with Horan, he mentioned that he had had 'one or two other paintings from Cooney the last year or two'."

"Hard quote?"

Flynn was holding the elevator door for him.

"Reasonably." Fletch stepped in.

Flynn pushed the button for the third floor.

"And you think those two other paintings he had from Cooney were the two de Grassi paintings that showed up in his catalogue?"

"What else is there to think?"

"Many things. One might think many other things."

On the third floor, they stepped out into a spacious, tasteful living room.

"Isn't this lovely?" said Flynn. "I can hardly blame the man for wanting to hold on to his possessions."

Flynn turned to Fletch.

"Now what, precisely, are we looking for?"

Fletch shrugged. "At this point, fifteen paintings and a Degas horse."

"The horse is a sculpture, I take it?"

"Yes."

"There's a sculpture of a ballerina on the first floor. . . ."

"Yes. That's a Degas," said Fletch.

"But it's not a horse. Saturday in your apartment, you said there were nineteen works in the de Grassi collection."

"Yes. Two have been sold through this gallery. A third, the Picasso, is downstairs. So there are fifteen paintings and the one sculpture."

"And do the works have anything in common?"

Flynn had walked them into a small, dark dining room.

"Not really. They belong to all sorts of different schools and eras. Many of them, but not all, are by Italian masters."

"This would be the kitchen, I think."

They looked in at white, gleaming cabinets and dark blue counters.

"Nothing in there, I think," said Flynn, "except some Warhols on the shelves."

Back in the living room, Flynn said, "Are you looking?"

"Yes."

There were some unimportant drawings behind the piano, and a large Mondrian over the divan.

Flynn snapped the light on in a small den off the living room. "Anything in here?"

A Sisley over the desk—the usual winding road and winding stream. The room was too dark for it.

"No."

"I rather like that one," said Flynn, looking at it closely. He turned away from it. "Ah, going around with you is an education."

They climbed the stairs to the fourth floor.

The houseman stood on the landing. Thin in his long, dark bathrobe, thin face long in genuine grief, he stood aside, obviously full of questions regarding the future of his master, his own future—questions his dignity prohibited he ask.

"Ah, yes," said Flynn.

In the bedroom was a shocking, life-sized nude—almost an illustration—of no quality whatsoever, except that it was arousing.

"The man had a private taste," said Flynn. "I suspect he entertained very few of his fellow faculty members in his bedroom."

One guest room had a collection of cartoons; the other a photography wall.

Fletch said, "You see, Inspector, Horan didn't really own paintings. Dealers don't. More than the average person, of course, a good deal more, in value, but a dealer is a dealer first, and a collector second."

"I see."

The houseman remained in the shadows of the corridor.

"Where is your room?" asked Flynn.

"Upstairs, sir."

"May we see it?"

The houseman opened a corridor door to a flight of stairs.

His bedroom was spartan : a bed, a bureau, a chair, a closet, a small television. His bath was spotless.

An attic room across the fifth floor landing contained nothing but the usual empty suitcases, trunks, a great many empty picture frames, a rolled rug, defunct lighting fixtures.

Flynn said, "Are the picture frames significant?"

"No."

Again on the third floor landing, Flynn said to the houseman, "Is there a safe in the house?"

"Yes, sir. In Mister Horan's office."

"You mean the wee one?"

"Yes, sir."

"I've already seen that. I guess I mean a vault. Is there a vault in the house, something of good, big size?"

"No, sir."

"You'd know if there were?"

"Yes, sir."

Flynn put his hand on the old man's forearm.

"I'm sorry for you. Have you been with him long?"

"Fourteen years."

The old man took a step back into the shadow.

"This must be quite a shock to you."

"It is, sir."

They took the elevator to the second floor and went through

the four galleries there. One was completely empty. The others had only a few works in each, lit and displayed magnificently.

Flynn said, "Nothing, eh?"

He might have been taking a Sunday stroll through a sculpture garden.

"I wouldn't say exactly nothing," said Fletch. "But none of the de Grassi paintings."

Despite the house's perfect climate control, Fletch's forehead was hot. His hands were sticky.

Flynn was in no hurry.

"Well, we'll go out to Weston now." Flynn buttoned his raincoat. "The Weston police will meet us at their border."

Double-parked, Grover waited outside in the black Ford.

"We'll both get in the back," said Flynn. "That way we can talk more easily."

Grover drove west on Newbury Street.

Fletch was sitting as far back in his dark corner as he could.

Coat opened again, knees wide, Flynn took up a great lot of room, anyway.

"Well," he said, "I guess I'll miss two o'clock feeding this morning. At least I know Elsbeth can't wait. Have you ever been to Weston?"

"No," said Fletch.

"Of course you haven't. You're a stranger in town. And we've been watching you as if you were a boy with a slingshot since you arrived. I hear it's a pretty place."

Flynn chuckled, in the dark.

"All this time poor Grover up there thought you were the guilty one. Eh, Grover?"

Sergeant Richard T. Whelan did not answer the bird's turd.

"Well," said Flynn, "so did I. More or less. When was it? Wednesday night, I think. I thought we were going to get a confession out of you. Instead, you invited us for dinner. Then that day on the phone, when I couldn't get around to see you, I felt sure I could convince you of your guilt. I decided I had to get to know this man. So on Saturday I invaded your privacy for the purpose of getting to know you—an old technique of mine—and damnall, you still turned up as innocent as a spring lamb."

They went down the ramp on to the Turnpike Extension and proceeded at a sedate pace, well below the speed limit.

"When I heard your voice on the phone early Sunday morning,

I thought sure you were calling from a bar ready to confess."
Flynn laughed. "Unburden your soul."

"I might yet," said Fletch.

Grover sat up to look at him through the rear-view mirror.

Still chuckling, Flynn said, "Now what do you mean by that?"

"I hate to spoil your time," said Fletch, "but Horan couldn't
have killed Ruth Fryer."

"Ah, but he did."

"How?"

"He hit her over the head with a whisky bottle. A full whisky
bottle."

"It doesn't make sense, Flynn."

"It does. It was his purpose to frame you."

"He didn't know me."

"He didn't have to. And, to a greater extent than you realize,
he did know you. Although you're a great investigative
reporter . . ."—Flynn took coins for the toll out of his pocket and
handed them to Grover— ". . . you made a mistake, lad."

"You have to pay tolls?"

"This road is in the state system, and I work for the city. We've
got enough governments in this country now to spread thinly
around the world."

"What mistake?"

"Matter of days after Count de Grassi is reported kidnapped,
then murdered, Horan gets this innocent wee letter, from Rome
of all places, asking him to locate one of the de Grassi paintings."

"He knew nothing about the de Grassi murder," Fletch said.
"The local papers didn't carry it. I checked."

"I did, too. Earlier today. So I asked the man tonight what
paper he reads, and he said the *New York Times*. The *Times* did
carry the story.

"Christ. I knew he read the *Times*."

"You had even been mentioned by name, as Peter Fletcher,
that is, as the de Grassi family spokesman the day you had the
ladies reveal their most intimate finances to convince the kidnappers they couldn't come up with the exorbitant ransom. The
Times printed it."

"Why would they have? From Italy?"

"You're the journalist. There's no end of interest in crime, my
lad."

"Ow."

"You were undone by the press, my lad. You're not the first."

"Horan would have noticed even a small item concerning the de Grassis."

"Precisely."

Fletch said, "He must be in cahoots with Cooney."

"I doubt any man would go to the extent Horan did to protect another man. It's possible, of course," Flynn said. "Anything's possible."

"It's still not possible."

"So you write him this innocent letter of enquiry from Rome, telling him which painting in all the world has caught your fancy, what day you'll arrive in Boston, and where you'll be staying.

"On the day you're due to arrive, the handsome, sauve, sophisticated Horan, probably with an empty suitcase, went to the airport, probably pretended he had just arrived from someplace, picks up the Trans World Airline Ground Hostess. . . ."

"I didn't tell him what airlines I was flying."

"If he knows what day you're arriving, he can find out what airlines, what flight number, and what arrival time with a single phone call. Surely you know that."

"Yes."

"As handsome a man as he is, looking as safe as your favourite uncle, he suggests Ruth Fryer join him for dinner, at some fancy place obviously he can afford. Probably he mentions he's a widower, an art dealer, on the Harvard faculty. Why wouldn't she go with him? Her boyfriend's not in town. She's in a city she doesn't know. Dinner with Horan sounds better than sitting in her motel room manicuring her fist."

"You haven't gotten to the impossibilities yet."

"There aren't any. Ach, another toll." He rummaged in his pocket again. "Don't they ever stop their infernal taxing?"

He handed more coins to Grover.

"He taxies Ms. Fryer to her motel. Allows her time to change. Waits for her in the bar. When she reappears, he has a drink all poured and waiting for her. He buys her more than one. It's his point to give you time to get into your apartment and out again. He's perfectly sure that you, a man alone in a strange city, an unfamiliar apartment, of course will take himself out to dinner. And you did."

Grover steered into the side road which curved up through the woods into Weston.

"Mister Horan was a pretty good predictor," Flynn said.

Ahead, a car was pulled off the road, showing only its parking lights.

"Is that a police car, Grover?"

"Yes, sir."

"They'd be waiting for us. Not only do they have to effect the warrant, but surely we'd never find the house by ourselves in this woodsy place."

Grover stopped behind the parked car.

"Using the excuse of dropping off his suitcase, I'm sure, Horan takes Ruth Fryer to what he says is his apartment, but which is really your apartment. An innocent enough excuse to get a girl home with you." A uniformed policeman from the other car was striding towards them. "You might remember it yourself."

"Flynn," Fletch said. "Horan didn't have a key to that apartment."

"Ah, but he did. A few years ago he arranged some restoration work on Bart Connors' paintings while the Connorses were vacationing in the Rockies. And who'd ever demand a key back from a man like Ronald Risom Horan, or even remember he had it?" Flynn rolled down the window. "You should see the number of keys in his desk. Hello!" he said through the window.

"He told me he had done restoration work for Connors."

"Inspector Flynn?"

"I am that."

"Weston Police, sir. You're here to enter the Horan house with a warrant?"

"We are."

Flynn was hunched forward, blocking the window.

"If you'll just follow us, sir."

"We will. And what is your name?"

"Officer Cabot, sir."

The policeman returned to his car, Flynn rolled up his window, and they started off in tandem at a slow pace.

Fletch said, "Well."

"You see, all the time you thought you were leading him down the garden path, he was leading you down the garden path."

"Because he reads the *Times*."

"You were a great threat to him. He had to get rid of you. If he murdered you outright, he'd be a natural suspect. You were coming to Boston to see him, and only him. So he contrived this magnificent circumstance to stop your investigation before it ever started. It's a good thing I didn't arrest you right away. Isn't it, Grover? The man must have been mighty surprised to have you show up the next day at his office as free as a birdie in an orchard."

"I'm grateful to you."

"Well, we got our man, although I had to withstand more than one tongue-lashing from that boyo up there in the front seat. Terrible tongue-lashings, they were."

They were going down the driveway.

"So Horan bopped the young lady over the head with a full bottle of whisky, before or after he tore the dress off her, put all the other liquor bottles away, put water in the carafe to make things as easy as possible for you to implicate yourself, knowing as sure as God made cats' eyes any man coming into a strange apartment at night finding a naked murdered girl would go to the nearest bottle and pour himself a big one."

"Except you."

"I might be tempted myself."

The uniformed policemen were waiting for them on the gravel.

"Here's the warrant," said Flynn.

Cabot said, "There was an attempted burglary here tonight."

"Was there, indeed?"

"Yes, sir."

"'Attempted', you say?"

"Yes, sir. The burglar or burglars didn't actually gain entry to the house. The alarm scared them away."

"And how do you know that already?"

"Mister Horan came out earlier. We went through the house with him. He said nothing was missing."

"Is that where he was? Now isn't that interesting? He said he was taking a ride in the moonlight. Now why didn't he tell me?"

Cabot said, "In fact, he was here when we arrived."

"Do you suppose he robbed himself?" Flynn squinted at Fletch. "Could he have known we were breathing down his neck?"

Fletch said, "How would I know?"

Flynn looked at Grover, helpless, and shrugged.

"Well, let's see what's inside."

On the porch, Officer Cabot put his hand through the frame of the broken window and pushed the plywood free. It clattered to the kitchen floor. He reached around, released the locks, and opened the door.

In the kitchen, they crunched on glass.

Turning on and off lights as they went, the five men went through the house, the dining room, the living room, the library.

The house was furnished in the worst country house style—ill-fitting, ersatz Colonial pine furniture, threadbare rugs which should have been retired long since.

At the top of the stairs on the second storey, Flynn turned to Fletch.

"Am I wrong, or is there nothing at all of value in this house?"

The uniformed policemen were turning on lights in the bedrooms.

Fletch said, "So far I've seen nothing of value."

Flynn said, "Then why the extensive, expensive burglar alarms?"

They went through the bedrooms. Again like the worst New England country houses, they were all furnished like boarding school dormitories. Everything was solid, cheap, simple and unattractive.

"From outside," said Flynn, "you'd think this an imposing country mansion, stuffed with the wealths of Persia. Any burglar attracted to this house would be a swimmer diving into a dry pool."

As they had proceeded, Flynn had opened and closed the doors to empty closets absently.

In the middle bedroom, in the rear of the second storey, he opened the closet door.

"Now, that's something. Look at the dust sheets, folded so neatly." He pulled the chain to the overhead light. "Not much dust on the floor spaces near the walls. There's a dust-free space in the centre of the floor, too. Do you see?"

Fletch looked over his shoulder.

"Do you think the paintings were here?"

"We'll never know."

He pulled the chain and closed the door.

Climbing the stairs to the attic, Flynn said to Officer Cabot, "Mister Horan was sure nothing was missing?"

"Yes, sir."

"You went through the house with him yourself, did you?"

"Yes, sir."

"Did you go through the closets in the bedrooms with him?"

"Yes, sir. Every one."

After they looked around the attic rooms, Flynn asked Officer Cabot, "And are burglaries common around here?"

"Yes."

The other policeman said, "Three on this road this month."

"Ah, things are getting to a terrible state."

Again standing on the back porch, waiting for the Weston policemen to close up the house, Flynn said, "I don't think the man Horan ever lived here at all. What was the house for?"

"Maybe he inherited it."

Slamming the door behind him, Officer Cabot gave Flynn a friendly nod.

"What shall we say if Mister Horan asks us why we searched his house?"

"Mister Horan won't be asking," said Flynn. "We arrested him earlier this evening for first degree murder."

They were driving east on the Turnpike Extension.

"It's a puzzle," said Flynn. "It is. How could he have known enough to rob himself? And what did he do with the paintings?"

Fletch said, "Perhaps you weren't very convincing as a man who wanted to sell a Ford Madox Brown."

"I spoke to him in German," said Flynn.

"Inspector, I still don't see that your evidence against Horan is any better than your evidence against me."

"It is. His fingerprints were all over your apartment."

"His? I asked you about fingerprints."

"And I told you that we had yours, Mrs. Sawyer's, Ruth Fryer's, and a man's we presumed to be Bart Connors'. We were never sure of the man's prints. Mister Connors, you see, has never been in the service and he's never been charged with any crime. His fingertips are as virginal as the day he was born. There is no record of his fingerprints. And all this time he's been enjoying your house in Italy."

"He certainly has."

"We had Mister Horan's fingerprints because he had been a Navy Commander, you know."

"I know."

"It wasn't until we were chatting over tea on Saturday and you allowed me to know why you were really in Boston—to see Mister Horan—that I considered we might try to match up the fingerprints we found in your apartment with those Mister Horan had on record. A perfect fit. He was a bit careless there. He thought he was so far removed from being a suspect for this particular crime, he never wiped up after himself. Even so, I suspect a more experienced policeman never would have suspected Mister Horan. Such a respectable man."

"Does he know you have his fingerprints?"

"Oh, yes. He's confessed."

"You finally have a confession. From someone."

"It's much easier when there's a confession. It cuts down on the department's court time."

The moon had disappeared.

Fletch said, "Lucy Connors didn't kill Ruth Fryer."

"Indeed not. She's as innocent as a guppy. You must get over your prejudices, lad."

"Did you know Horan was guilty this afternoon when I was talking to you? I mean, yesterday afternoon? In your office."

"Yes, lad. I'm sorry to say I deceived you something terrible. There I was, a wee lad again in Germany, asking you for your autograph while I took your picture to send on to London. By five o'clock yesterday we had matched up Horan's prints with those in your apartment, and I had made an appointment to see him. The warrants were in process."

"Flynn. Have you ever felt stupid?"

"Oh, yes. A cup of tea is a great help."

Flynn gave Grover money for another toll.

"Good luck on the City Councilperson's murder," Fletch said.

"Ach, that's over, all this long time."

"Is it?"

"Sure, I'm just letting the politicians exercise their bumps so they'll accept the solution when I give it to them. They so want to think the crime is political. They've all demanded police protection, you know. It makes them look so much grander when they go through the streets with a cop at their heels."

"Who did it?"

"Did you say, 'Who did it'?"

"Yes."

"Well, you have your humour yourself, don't you? Her husband did it. A poor, meek little man who's been in the back seat of that marriage since they pulled away from the church."

"How do you know he did it?"

"I found the man who sold him the ice pick. A conscientious Republican, to boot. An unimpeachable witness, with the evidence he has, in a case involving Democrats."

Outside 152 Beacon Street, before getting out of the car, Fletch put his hand out to Flynn.

"I've met a great cop," he said.

They shook hands.

"I'm coming along slowly," said Flynn. "I'm learning. Bit by bit."

XXXIX

TEN-THIRTY Tuesday morning the buzzer to the downstairs door sounded.

Fletch gave his button a prolonged answering push to give his guest ample time to enter.

He opened the front door to his apartment and went into the kitchen.

Coming back across the hall with the coffee tray he heard the elevator creaking slowly to the sixth floor.

He put the tray on the coffee table between the two divans.

When he returned to the foyer, his guest, nearly seventy, in a dark overcoat, brown suit a little too big for him, grey bags under his eyes making him no less distinguished, was standing hesitantly in the hall.

Fletch aid, "Hi, Menti."

As he shook hands, the man's smile was dazzling, despite the lines of concern in his face.

"I never knew you wear false teeth," Fletch said.

Taking his guest's coat and putting it in a closet, Fletch said, "They found your body a few days ago in a pasture outside Turin."

Clasping his hands together, the guest entered the living room and allowed himself to be escorted to a divan. Count Clementi Arbogastes de Grassi was not accustomed to a cold climate.

He sipped a cup of coffee and crossed his legs. "My friend," he said.

Fletch was comfortable with his coffee in the other divan.

"Now I ask you the saddest question I have ever had to ask any man in my life." The Count paused. "Who stole my paintings? My wife? Or my daughter?"

Fletch sipped from his cup.

184

"Your daughter. Andy. Angela."

Menti sat, cup and saucer in one hand in his lap, staring at the floor for several moments.

"I'm sorry, Menti."

Fletch finished his coffee and put the cup and saucer on the table.

"I knew it had to be one of them who arranged it," Menti said. "For the paintings to have been stolen on our honeymoon. The theft at that time was too significant. The paintings had been there for decades. The house was usually empty, except for Ria and Pep. Few knew the paintings were there. But Sylvia was with me in Austria and Angela was here in school."

"I know."

Menti sat up and put his unfinished coffee on the table.

"Thank you for being my friend, Fletch. Thank you for helping me to find out."

"Were you comfortable enough in captivity?"

"You arranged everything splendidly. I rather enjoyed being a retired Italo-American on the Canary Islands. I made friends."

"Of course."

"Where are the ladies now? Sylvia and Angela?"

"They flew the coop this morning. No note. No anything."

"What does 'flew the coop' mean?"

"They left. Quickly."

"They were here?"

"Yes."

"Both of them?"

"Under the very same roof."

"Why did they leave, 'flew the coop'?"

"Either they both left together, or Andy left when she heard Horan was arrested, and Sylvia took off after her. It must have been quite a scene. Sorry I missed it."

The Count said, "Are they both well?"

"Grieving, of course, but otherwise fine." He poured warm coffee into the Count's half-empty cup. "I have fifteen of the paintings. Two have been sold, you know. The police are keeping one, the big Picasso, 'Vino, Viola, Mademoiselle', as evidence. You'll probably never get it back without spending three times the painting's financial worth in legal fees, taxes, international wrangling and what have you. And we have the Degas horse."

Menti absently turned the cup in its saucer.

"Everything is in a truck, downstairs," Fletch said. "You and

I can leave for New York as soon as you get warmed up."

Menti sat back, sad and tired.

"Why did she do it?"

"Love. Love for you. I don't think Andy cared that much about the paintings. She doesn't care about the money.

"When her mother died," Fletch continued, "Andy, as a little girl, thought she would take her mother's place in your affection. You remarried. She has told me how heartbroken she was, and furious. She was fourteen. When your second wife left you, she was pleased. She thought you had learned your lesson. Because you had been married in France, you could divorce. Then, while Andy was in school here, you married Sylvia. Andy was no longer a little girl. She was old enough to express her rage. In her eyes, you had kept something from her all these years. She took something from you. The de Grassi Collection."

"She wasn't afraid Sylvia might have inherited them?"

"I'm not sure, but I have the impression Andy knew that under Italian law children of the deceased have to inherit at least a third of the estate. Have I got that right? I'm sure Sylvia had no idea of that. Knowledge of the law could have motivated either one of them to steal the paintings—from the other."

"Angela wanted the whole collection."

"I guess so. She doesn't expect much sense of family from Sylvia. People like Ria and Pep are very important to Andy."

"But how did she do it? A little girl, like that?"

"It took me a while to make the connection. I knew Andy had been to school in this country. I hadn't realized her school was here in Boston, or Cambridge, which is just across the river. I knew her school was Radcliffe. I didn't realize that Radcliffe is joined with Harvard. Radcliffe women now receive Harvard degrees. Horan, the Boston art dealer, was Andy's professor at Harvard."

"I see. But I think it would be difficult to get your professor to commit a grand, international robbery for you because you didn't like your father marrying again, no?"

"One would think so. However, Horan, who had gotten used to a very expensive way of life, was going broke."

"You know he was broke?"

"Yes. Five years ago he sold his wife's famous jewel, the Star of Hunan jade, to an Iranian. I knew that before I came here."

"Still . . . such a distinguished man."

"He's also a handsome, sophisticated man, Menti. An older

man. For years, Andy had been wanting a certain kind of attention from you...."

Menti's eyes were dull as they gazed at Fletch. "You believe their relationship was more intimate than is usual between a student and teacher?"

"I suspect so. For one purpose or another."

"I see." Menti sipped his coffee. "It happens. So, Fletcher, it was Horan who actually arranged for the paintings to be stolen."

"Yes. You showed me the catalogues from the Horan Gallery. Two of the de Grassi paintings were being sold, or, in fact, had been sold. We made our plan. We left copies of the catalogues for each of the ladies to find.

"Andy was enraged," Fletch said. "She knew Horan had the paintings, of course. She was enraged that he was selling them without her. Did Sylvia react at all?"

Menti said, "She never looked in the catalogues. I couldn't get her to." Menti chuckled lightly and shook his head. "When you called from Cagna saying you were driving down with an upset Angela, it was too late. I could wait no longer for Sylvia to notice. I had to go forward with our plan and get kidnapped."

"I don't know what Andy was really thinking on that drive to Livorno. She was certainly going to you, maybe to confess. More likely, she didn't know what she was doing."

"My disappearance helped clarify things," Menti said.

"Yes. Essentially, Andy sent me here to find the paintings so she could steal them back from Horan. She probably wouldn't have played her own hand out, unless she thought you were dead." Fletch swallowed coffee. "This morning Horan was arrested. Exit Andy. Exit Sylvia."

"Enter Menti."

The buzzer to the downstairs door sounded.

"We're taking the paintings to a dealer in New York. A man I trust implicitly." Fletch stood up to answer the door. "His name is Kasner. On East 66th Street."

In the foyer, he shouted into the mouthpiece, "Who is it?"

The answering voice was so soft it took Fletch a moment to assimilate what it said.

"Francis Flynn, Mister Fletcher."

"Oh! Inspector?"

"The same."

Fletch pressed the button that would release the lock on the door downstairs.

Quickly, he grabbed Menti's coat from the closet.

Then he went into the den and took the truck keys from a drawer of the desk.

In the living room, he handed the coat and keys to Menti.

"Hurry up," he said. "Put on your coat. The man who is coming up is a policeman."

Moving gracefully, with speed, Menti stood up and put on the coat Fletch held for him.

"I won't be able to drive to New York with you, Menti. Can you make the trip alone?"

"Of course."

"Here are the keys. It's a black caravan truck, a Chevrolet, parked at the curb outside the apartment house, I think, to the right as you leave the building. The licence plate on it is R99420. Have you got it?"

"In general, yes."

"Kasner's address is 20 East 66th Street, New York."

"I can remember."

"He's expecting you this afternoon. Come into the foyer with me, as if you were leaving, anyway."

The doorbell rang.

"Good morning, Inspector."

"Good morning, Mister Fletcher."

The little face on top of the huge body was bright and shining from a recent close shave. The green eyes were beaming like a cat's.

Fletch brought Menti forward by the elbow.

"I'd like you to meet a friend, from Italy, who just stopped by. Inspector Flynn, this is Giuseppe Grochola."

Flynn's eyes went to Menti. He put out his hand.

"Count Clementi Arbogastes de Grassi, is it?"

Menti hesitated not at all before shaking hands.

"Pleased to meet you, Inspector."

Flynn said to Fletch, "I never forget a thing I've heard. Isn't it marvellous?"

"It's marvellous, Flynn."

"And such a great cop I am, too. Didn't I hear someone say that?"

"You did, Inspector."

"Now why do you suppose this man who's supposed to be dead,

this Count Clementi Arbogastes de Grassi, is standing here in your front hall?"

"I'm on my way to the airport, Inspector."

Fletch said, "He's been found, Flynn. Isn't that great?"

"It's a wonder he was lost at all."

"A narrow escape," said Fletch.

"It's a confusion," said Menti. "I came here to see my wife and daughter. They, hearing I was found alive, rushed off to Rome, not knowing I was coming here."

"I see," said Flynn. "And how was it, to be dead?"

Menti said, "I'm trying to catch them at the airport, Inspector."

Flynn stood away from the door.

"I'd never come between a man and his family," he said. "Have a joyful reunion."

Fletch opened the door.

"There's some coffee in the living room, Inspector."

He opened the elevator door for Menti.

Flynn had wandered into the living room.

Fletch whispered, "Send me back the licence plates. By mail."

From inside the elevator, Menti whispered, "What do I do with the truck?"

"Leave it anywhere. It will get stolen."

Still in his overcoat, Flynn stood over the coffee table.

"There's not an unused cup," he said, "on this brisk morning."

"I'll get one."

"Never mind. I had my tea."

"I wasn't expecting you," Fletch said.

"I suspected as much. I'm only here for the moment. I thought I'd ask you this morning if you've had any ideas at all as to where the de Grassi paintings might be?"

"I've just been through that, Inspector."

"Have you?"

"I told Menti everything."

"You must have been mighty surprised to see him."

"Mighty."

"The ladies have gone already, have they?"

"They were gone when I got back. They must have gotten the news during the night, while I was with you."

"And they didn't wait for you? Your girlfriend and the Countess."

"Menti's discovery was big news, Inspector."

"I daresay it was. And how was he found?"

"Wandering near the steps of Saint Sebastian."

"In a daze, was he?"

"No. He'd been let out of a car."

"Remarkable they'd feed a captive that long. Italian kidnappers must have hearts of honey. A month or more, wasn't it?"

"About that."

"Well, anything is possible under the sun." Flynn turned on his heel at the end of the room. "Now, where do you suppose the paintings are this morning?"

"Well, Inspector, you might believe Horan hid them last night."

"I might believe that, yes. The man doesn't say so himself."

"You asked him?"

"I did, yes."

"But, Inspector, who can believe a murderer?"

"Ach, now there's a point worthy of my own Jesuit training."

"What did Horan say, precisely?"

"The man says he never heard of the paintings."

"Didn't he say a man named Cooney in Texas has them?"

"He says he never heard of a man named Cooney."

"It's a great puzzle, Inspector."

"It is that. The man must have had the paintings, or he never would have gone to the extent of murder to frame and thus dispose of you."

"Perhaps he just doesn't like people named Peter."

"I'll ask him that." Flynn, hands behind back, walked back down the room. "I'd almost think you took them yourself, Fletch. There was a burglary at the man's house last night. If the man hadn't gone out there immediately afterwards and told the police nothing was missing."

"I suppose I could make some tea," Fletch said. "The water's still hot."

"No, I must be going." Flynn headed towards the front door. "Of course, a man may be reluctant to admit something he isn't supposed to have is stolen from him. I mean, how would a man say something I stole was stolen from me?"

Fletch said, "I understand reluctance, Inspector."

"Ach," said Flynn. "A man has no privacy at all."

Before he opened the front door, Flynn turned to Fletch, and said, "Which reminds me, Mister Fletcher. Finally we discovered what else you did on that Wednesday you went in one door of the Ritz and out of the other."

"Oh?"

"You bought a truck. The marvellous bureaucracy dropped the registration into my hands just this morning."

Flynn began to rummage in all his pockets at once.

"Now, why would you buy a truck and rent a car the same day?"

"I was going to use it for skiing, Inspector."

"Ach! That's a perfectly good answer. What do you mean, you *were* going to use it for skiing?"

"It was stolen. I've been meaning to report it."

"Ah, Mister Fletcher. You should report such things. And when was it stolen?"

"Almost immediately."

"What a pity. That very afternoon? Is that why you rented the car?"

"I didn't want to have to drive a truck around town."

"Gracious, yes, indeed. I was forgetting about the man's style."

"It was stolen a day or two later. I had parked it on the street."

"Terrible lot of crime around these days, isn't there? The police should do something." Flynn pulled a slip of paper from one of his pockets. "Ah, here's the little darling. A light blue Chevrolet van truck, last year's model, licence number 671-773. Is that it?"

"That's it."

"Just the right size truck, I'd say, for transportin' paintings and a sculptured horse."

Fletch said, "Skis, too."

Flynn said, "Do you suppose Horan stole it himself, for the purpose of stealing the de Grassi paintings away from himself?"

"Anything's possible, Inspector. He may have committed that crime, too, and blocked it out."

"Highly unlikely, I'd say."

Flynn opened the door.

"Well, I'll put out an all-points bulletin on this truck immediately. Light blue Chevrolet caravan truck, last year's model, licence number 671-773. Seeing you're a friend, been such a help on the terribly difficult case, I'll put the screws to the boyos statewide. There's no chance this truck won't be picked up in a matter of hours."

"Very good of you, Inspector."

"Tut. Think nothing of it. Anything for a friend."

Fletch closed the front door, diminishing the sound of the descending elevator.

His watch said fifteen minutes to twelve. Tuesday.

He was almost perfectly a week late.

In the den, he picked up the phone and dialled a number he had looked up and memorized in the airport the previous Tuesday.

While he was waiting for the number to answer, he pushed the drape aside with his hand and looked down into the street.

Menti was just climbing down from the back of the truck.

He had been looking at the paintings!

"Hurry up, Menti," Fletch said to the windowpane. "For Pete's sake!"

"Hello? 555-2301."

Menti was unlocking the driver's side door of the truck.

"Hello?" the voice said.

"Hello," said Fletch.

He craned his neck. He could see the top of Flynn's head as he walked out of the apartment building.

Menti was in the truck.

"Yes, hello?" the voice said.

"I'm sorry," said Fletch. "Is this the Tharp Family Foundation?"

Flynn was getting into the passenger seat of a black Ford.

"Yes, sir."

Exhaust was coming from the tailpipes of both the police car and the truck.

"May I speak with your director, please?"

"Who shall I say is calling, please?"

The double-parked police car began to move forward.

Without looking, Menti darted out of his parking space with the bounce and jerk people make when unaccustomed to driving a vehicle.

The police car braked hard, making the front end of its chassis bob towards the road surface.

"Sir? Who shall I say is calling?"

Apparently, the driver of the police car waved ahead the black Chevrolet van truck, last year's model, licence number R99420.

The two vehicles proceeded up the street, the black police car behind the black, jerking truck.

Fletch released the window drape.

"I'm sorry. This is Peter Fletcher. . . ."